P9-CEA-199

YESTERDAY'S HORSES

Yesterday's Horses

JEAN SLAUGHTER DOTY

Macmillan Publishing Company

New York

I'd like to acknowledge, with many thanks, the interest and kindness of Dr. Alfred Prince, and of Dorcas MacClintock, Curator Affiliate, Yale Peabody Museum of Natural History, during the preparation of this book.

I am extremely grateful for their technical advice and encouragement, but I take full responsibility for the story, which is mine alone.

—J. S. D.

Macmillan Publishing Company
866 Third Avenue, New York, N.Y. 10022
Collier Macmillan Canada, Inc.
Printed in the United States of America
10 9 8 7 6 5 4 3 2 1

LIBRARY OF CONGRESS CATALOGING IN PUBLICATION DATA
Doty, Jean Slaughter, date.
Yesterday's horses.

Summary: While riding in the mountains, Kelly finds an orphaned foal that seems to belong to a breed of wild horses supposedly extinct for thousands of years and which holds the secret to a modern medical mystery.
1. Children's stories, American. [1. Horses—Fiction. 2. Veterinarians—Fiction] I. Title.
PZ7.D7378Ye 1985 [Fic] 84-42981
ISBN 0-02-733040-0

To Kit—
for her encouragement and support,
from the very beginning

Chapter One

The bridle path was rough and uneven. There were tumbled rocks I'd never seen before, and fallen trees were scattered at uneven angles where a few tremendous boulders clogged the path. My chestnut horse, Rusty, snorted and blew through his nostrils as he did his best to pick his way through. He seemed as surprised as I was at the changes that the past winter had made. This was our first ride out into the mountains since last fall.

I shortened my reins and he stopped with relief. I patted his red-gold neck apologetically. We'd gone far enough. I should have let him stop long before this.

The winter had been savage and wild all through the Northwest. Terrible storms had beaten the far western slopes of the mountains, blown over the peaks, and screamed down into our valley. Blizzards had closed the roads for days at a time. The cold had lasted late into the spring, and then sudden warmth had spilled over the mountains and freed the ice and snow.

The mountain and valley streams sang and then roared over their banks as the abrupt thaw melted the ice and snow in a rush. The quiet stream at the northern border of our farm turned into an angry turmoil of mud and sliding rocks. Broken trees and branches washed down from the mountain, piled against the willows, ripped out the footbridge, and tore it away.

Then it was over. The crazy late spring brought grass to blazing green life in the fields almost overnight, it seemed. Buds foamed into pink blossoms on the branches of the apple trees. The streams settled back in their beds. Our small farm and orchard, and all the surrounding countryside, looked serene and pretty again.

But up on the mountain slopes, where Rusty and I were that morning, most of our favorite, friendly bridle paths had disappeared. The trees brought down by the winter storms, and the rocks pushed down the mountain by the ice and sudden thaw, had made a mess of everything. It wasn't much fun trying to struggle through the jumble of thick new undergrowth around all the confusion on the paths.

I was riding without a saddle, and when Rusty jumped sideways suddenly, I nearly went off. I clutched at his red mane and just managed to stay on. I caught my breath from the surprise and untangled the reins from Rusty's mane. He was standing still now with his head high and his ears strained forward. He'd broken out in a light sweat that gleamed on his neck in the splashy sunlight that came through the thick tree branches over our heads.

"Rusty," I said in a low voice, "let's go home." The trees were pressing in around us with almost a threatening feeling. Rusty's nervousness was catching.

I shivered. I wished I hadn't come up here alone. My best friend, Lori, with her pretty brown Welsh pony, Rima, and her older brother, Mark, on his tall gray horse, Pennant, often rode with me on Saturday afternoons. We'd planned to ride out here on the mountain together today. But Lori had called earlier to tell me that Rima hadn't finished her breakfast grain that morning and didn't seem to feel well, and Mark's father had asked Mark to lend a hand with some work that, because of the late spring, hadn't yet been done on their farm. We'd agreed to wait for another time, but I was tired of riding Rusty in the same old places and had decided to come up to the mountain, anyway. Mom didn't much like me to ride up here by myself, though she'd never actually come out and forbidden it. I was now convinced she was right and started to turn Rusty back down the path the way we'd come. If I did any more exploring through the new wilderness the winter had slashed across the mountain, I decided I'd wait until I had company again.

Rusty didn't move. His hoofs, with their neat white socks above them, were braced on the path. His ears were pricked forward, though I could hear nothing but silence around us and ahead of us. Rusty's head was high and his nostrils were flaring.

"Come on, Rusty," I said impatiently. "Let's split." I looked down to speak to Kim, my black Border Collie, who always stayed close beside me when I rode. But for the first time I could ever remember, Kim had vanished.

I whistled sharply. "Come on, Kim," I called. "Let's go back." I heard him give an answering bark, but I couldn't see him anywhere.

Kim barked again, somewhere ahead of us where the path turned to wind up the side of the mountain. There was no way Rusty was going to take a single step forward. I tried to urge him on, pressing his sides strongly with my legs and heels, but Rusty only snorted stubbornly and braced himself even more stiffly in the path.

I gave a shaky sigh. I couldn't turn away and leave Kim. Maybe he had a paw caught between two rocks—maybe he'd gotten himself squeezed under a fallen tree branch and couldn't get away. Rusty was giving me no choice. I'd have to go to Kim on foot.

I slipped off Rusty's back, tied his reins to a low branch, and followed the remnants of the bridle path ahead. The leather soles of my boots slid on the rocks, and undergrowth tugged at my jeans. Cracked branches dangled from the trees close by the path. I ducked my head and pushed my way through.

The pathway turned abruptly to the left beside a towering rock ledge. I whistled to Kim again and practically fell over him at the same time. He was lying across the path. He wagged his white-tipped tail but didn't move. He was staring into the shadows of the undergrowth next to the wall of rock.

I knelt beside him to make sure he was all right. He wagged his tail again, and his white ruff shone as he turned his head briefly to lick my hand before looking back into the shadows again.

I stayed motionless where I was, kneeling beside

him, and tried to see what it was he was looking at with such intensity. I gave a jump of surprise—from under a deep tangle of vines and broken branches, two bright black eyes stared back at me.

I blinked and tried to sort shapes out of the shadows. I was looking at a foal or a very young horse of some kind, so bound up in the jumble of vines and freshly fallen tree branches that it couldn't move. The foal was a sandy brown, what I could see of it, with small tan ears, a pale dusty-brown muzzle, and a short black mane.

I sat back on my heels. I was stunned and bewildered. What was such a young thing doing up here on the mountain, all alone? Surely if anyone in the area had lost a foal, Mom or I would have heard of it. Anyway, I knew just about every horse and pony for miles around. No one I knew had a sandy dun horse or pony of any kind, young or old.

The foal struggled a few moments and gave up again. It was tired, I could tell. There was no way of knowing how long it had been trapped up here, all by itself.

"Here's a howdy do," I said out loud to Kim. He sat up enthusiastically. He expected, of course, that I'd rush right in to rescue the trapped foal. . . . The longer I looked at it, the surer I was that it was quite young.

I owned a good red pocket knife that would have been a terrific help. But it was in the pocket of my windbreaker back at the house. Not much use to me now.

Kim was right. I wasn't going to leave the foal alone up here to die. But I didn't know how I was going to rescue it, either.

Chapter Two

I got to my feet and approached the trapped foal gently. It started to struggle wildly again against the vines wrapped around its slim black legs. I half hoped it would suddenly free itself, but it had no more energy left to fight. Its head sagged against the ground.

I took a deep, shuddering breath and went to work.

I pulled at the tough vines that held the foal. They were too strong for me to break. I searched the path for a stone with a sharp edge I might be able to use for a knife, and that's how I discovered the foal's dead mother.

She was almost completely hidden under a fallen tree beside the path. The tree had come down on her not long before; the earth clinging to its roots was still damp and hadn't yet started to dry. It looked as though the small dun mare had died a quick and merciful death. I certainly hoped so. From what I could make out under the crushed branches of the fallen tree, she was the same sandy brown as her foal, though only her head, with its mealy tan muzzle, and part of her neck and body showed clearly. Her head was an unusual wedge shape, with broad, flat cheekbones. She had the same short, black mane and black-rimmed ears as the foal. She had the same dark oval eyes, too, but hers were staring unseeingly at the bright sky above her. I touched her gently, but she didn't move; her body was already beginning to cool. I covered her as well as I could with scraps of broken branches, ferns, and leaves, before I went back to the trapped orphan.

"I guess I'm elected to be your momma now," I said to it gently. "I'll get you out of here, one way or another. Not to worry."

The foal had enough energy left to put its ears back and snap at me when I went close to its head. "Neat," I said. "I'm only trying to help."

I found a thin rock with a reasonably sharp edge and sawed at the vines, dodging the foal's teeth and then its kicks as I slowly started to make some progress.

"I'm going to have problems with you, I can see

that," I said to the foal at last. "I'll have you free in a few more minutes, and then what? I've got to get you home to take care of you, and once you're untangled from all this, I don't think I'll ever get near you again."

On tired legs I went back to Rusty, unbuckled one of his reins, and went back up the slope to the helpless foal. I made a makeshift halter out of the rein, and gave the soft leather an extra loop around the foal's muzzle to stop it from biting at me while I went on with my work.

I was able to cut through some of the vines. Others I managed to twist out of the way and pull away from its legs. I don't know how long it took and it was hard work, but I was grimly determined to save the poor thing, no matter what. Kim sat and watched, panting with contented approval.

"Easy for you to look so pleased," I said to the dog. "If you were any use at all, you'd help and chew through some of this stuff, like the dogs do in movies and on television."

Kim wagged his tail again, which was his way of helping. I patted him and went back to work.

At last I was done. I pushed my hair back from my sweaty forehead with one hand while I hung onto the halter I'd made with the other. I was faced now with a whole new problem.

"How do you propose I go about getting this foal all the way home?" I asked Kim, as though I expected him to give me an answer. "It's not like finding a little lost lamb, you know. At least I could carry a lost lamb home on Rusty's back." Kim wagged his tail and looked at me adoringly.

"In any event," I said to the dog sternly, "the foal may well be hurt. I can't tell. Then what?" I sat down to rest for a few minutes. The foal hadn't yet tried to get to its feet, though I kept a tight hold of the rein I'd made into a halter in case it did.

Light was beginning to drain from the mountain. I couldn't wait much longer. Things were going to be tough enough without coping with dim twilight this deep in the woods.

I took a strong hold of the halter and gave it a firm pull. "Up," I said. "Come on, you've got to stand up if you can."

I coaxed and tugged on the halter. Kim nuzzled the foal's hindquarters and dodged cleverly out of the way when it kicked. The foal staggered to its feet at last. It swayed uncertainly as it balanced on the uneven ground, but I was thankful to see it was carrying its weight evenly on all four of its thin legs. It took another quick kick at Kim and switched its short tail, so it looked as though its back hadn't been hurt.

I'd been right; it was young, but not a baby. "I think," I said to it slowly, as I saw it standing for the first time, "you've got to be the funniest-looking foal I've ever seen. Never mind, it doesn't matter. With those black stripes on the top parts of your legs, maybe you're part zebra?" The foal, which I could now tell was a filly, put her ears back and glared at me fiercely.

"Forget it," I said. "This is only the beginning. Now we've got to get you home."

I pulled, Kim barked and herded from behind, and somehow we got the foal past her poor dead mother and onto a smoother part of the bridle path. I was sure I'd never have been able to handle it if the foal hadn't been worn out, but Kim and I together managed somehow while I wondered how I was going to lead both Rusty and the reluctant foal home.

I needn't have worried about Rusty. Maybe he caught the scent of the foal's dam lying dead under the broken tree, or panicked at the crashing sounds we made as we forced our way back down the mountain. Whatever the reason, I heard him give a whistling snort. He reared and flew back against his bridle. The bridle broke and Rusty raced away from us, tail in the air, going at a flying gallop down the path toward the farm.

There was no way I could catch him. I picked up the bridle and tucked it under my belt. With Kim's help from behind, the foal and I stumbled our way down the mountain.

I suppose I've taken longer trips. But no trip ever had seemed longer than this one with the tired but stubborn filly who fought and resisted every step of the way.

When we finally got back to the stable, Rusty was waiting patiently outside his stall door, as I'd expected he would be. I put the weary foal in the next stall, shut Rusty in his, and collapsed on an overturned bucket to catch my breath. Kim flopped down beside me in the stable aisle. Eventually I got myself a Coke from the refrigerator in the house. I went back to the stable and sat on the bucket again. The foal lay down in the sweet shavings bedding her stall, and Rusty made gentle nickering sounds, reminding me it was getting near his feeding time.

I looked wearily at Kim. "I hope to goodness this new little creature is weaned," I said, "and can handle regular food."

I knew Mom kept canned milk and bottles and all the other supplies needed for orphan foals in a cabinet in her office, just in case, but she kept a drum of little foal feed pellets in her office, too, and from the feel of the few bites the foal had already given me, I was sure she had plenty of teeth. I'd offer her the pellets first, I decided, and scrape up the energy to mix the formula only if it was needed.

Weary as the foal was, she was frightened of her new surroundings and scrambled quickly to her feet at every new sound. I moved as quietly as I could, filled and hung a bucket of fresh water in the stall, added an armful of good hay in case she was old enough to eat it, and fed Rusty his regular grain and hay.

When I was done with Rusty, the foal was lying down again but nibbling hungrily on the hay near her. I put some foal pellets in a shallow feed tub and went back into the stall.

The foal seemed to have lost some of her fear of me. I knelt near her head and gently offered the scattering of pellets in the feed tub. It was wonderful, after the first suspicious snorts, to see the dusty tan muzzle searching for each pellet, and the foal even let me touch her head as she ate.

I brushed Rusty, made sure his water bucket was full, and called to Kim.

"Nothing more we can do now," I said to the dog, firmly shutting the stable door. "Our discovery is tired, and all we can do now is let her rest, poor thing. Rusty's fine for the night. Enough. Let's go get some supper for ourselves."

Chapter Three

The phone rang in the kitchen just after I'd fed Kim. It was Mom, sounding as tired as I felt.

"I'll be late getting back," she said. "I've been to see Lori's Rima, and the pony isn't at all well. Now I'm at the Brewster farm with one of their Clydesdales—he's a very sick horse, and I don't want to leave him."

"That's awful," I said. "What's he got? Colic?"

"Not this time," said Mom. "He's running a very high fever. I'm trying to get it down. You go ahead and make yourself some supper. I'll eat whenever I can."

"Take care," I said sympathetically. Mr. Brewster's matched team of four huge Clydesdales was the pride of the entire valley. I'd often been to the Brewster farm, riding over on Rusty or going with Mom when she made her calls, and I never missed stopping to admire the huge bay horses either out in their pasture or in their enormous stalls. Mr. Brewster always led the Fourth of July parade with his magnificent gentle giants pulling a wagon full of delighted children. The brass buckles and medallions on the horses' harness were always sparkling with fresh polish, and the big round brass bells they wore made a deep, throaty sound with every dignified step the horses took.

Mom was a veterinarian and cared for most of the large farm animals in the area. She wasn't very tall and had short red curly hair, just a bit darker than mine—it had been a super shock when she'd first come to the valley. Everyone thought at first she'd come just to help my grandfather drive his mobile veterinary unit, after he'd been injured by a cow he was treating.

But Mom was a real vet, and a good one. She'd practiced for several years with a clinic near New York, doing most of her work with racehorses at the surrounding tracks.

We'd lived near New York then, too. But I'd always loved every minute of the few times we'd flown out to the Northwest to visit my grandfather on his small farm in the valley.

The valley itself was the shape of a raindrop, with the narrow part at the north end, where the farm was. Grandfather was too busy with his veterinary practice to do much farming himself, but it was still a neat place, with its open fields, its small apple orchard, the bright stream, and the mountains rising at the back.

My dad was Grandfather's only child. Dad was a geologist and traveled a lot, exploring fantastic parts of the world. He'd been packing for a trip to the Antarctic, with down jackets and weird-looking cameras and pieces of strange equipment scattered all over our apartment, the day Grandfather's letter had come. Dad had read it out loud to Mom and me at dinner that night.

" 'I've been put out of commission by a cow, if you can believe it,' " my grandfather wrote. " 'She banged me up pretty well. The local doc says I've got to take it easy for a few weeks while my leg and hip heal.

" 'I've got to look for a good vet to take over my practice temporarily. Why don't all of you come on out for a while and let Susan do something else besides treat those expensive toys of hers?' "

Mom laughed. The "expensive toys" she treated at the clinic and at the tracks were worth hundreds of thousands of dollars; some of the horses were worth more than a million. Each. There'd been rumors that Mom was about to be offered a partnership with the three other vets who ran the clinic. This was hardly the time for her to ask for a leave of absence.

Dad smiled and went on reading. " 'I'll go down to Florida to stay with an old buddy of mine and do some serious fishing, once I find the right kind of vet to help me out here.' "

Dad smiled at Mom again. "You know what that means, Susan. Cows," he said. "Sheep, too, as I remember. And pigs. Some horses and ponies. There are a few pretty fancy horse-breeding farms in the valley, but they're down at the south end, and there's a clinic of vets there that has the care of those quality horses pretty well sewn up."

"Mmmm," said Mom.

" 'Give me a call when you decide,' " Grandad finished in his letter.

Mom turned to look out the apartment window at the lights on the highways, the traffic, and the buildings everywhere.

"You know something funny?" she said. "I'd really like to go."

"You won't have an operating room, or ultrasound equipment, like your hospital here, you know," Dad said. "You'd be working with no more than a mobile unit, in all kinds of weather, and an office and a treatment room in a wing off the house.

But you know all that, of course. You've been there. You've seen it."

Dad wore a beard that matched his sandy hair and he looked like a college professor, but he loved the excitement and challenge of the exploring he did. "No routine office work or teaching at a desk for me, not yet," he'd said often in the past. Now he said, "Susan, if you want to go, I'd certainly understand. Kelly could always stay here in the East and go to boarding school, if she'd rather."

I stared at him in shock until I saw him wink and grin at me. He was only joking. I smiled back. School was almost over for the summer, anyway, which he knew perfectly well. I couldn't think of anywhere I'd rather be than on the farm with Mom. Dad would be away, though there was plenty of room for him in Grandfather's rambling white house if he came home from the Antarctic while we were still there. No problem.

But it was up to Mom.

"Patching up racehorses isn't all there is to veterinary medicine," Mom said, half to herself. "It pays well, but it can get a little monotonous. . . ."

I almost bit a hole in my tongue to keep myself quiet.

Mom turned to smile at Dad and me, and her blue eyes were bright with excitement. "I really think I want to do it. I'm not sure the clinic will ever understand, but there it is. I wonder how long your father would need me?"

Dad glanced down at the letter in his hand. "He doesn't say. You know Dad. He doesn't go into much detail about his injuries or how long it might be before he can tackle his practice again. I guess you'd have to say it would be for an indefinite period of time."

"I don't care." Mom threw her hands in the air. "What a marvelous adventure this would be."

"Maybe you should think about it," Dad said.

"I'm sure I should," said Mom. "But there's really not much to think about, is there? It's only for a short time, a temporary break—it's not that big a decision. I have at least a month of vacation time coming. Why shouldn't I go to help your father? If the clinic here doesn't like it—"

"—they can stuff it," I finished her sentence for her with a grin I couldn't hold back any longer.

Phone calls flew back and forth. Before the evening was over, everything was set. I went to bed at least an hour later than usual. Not that this really mattered—it was Friday, so I had no homework I had to get done right away, and I could even sleep late the next morning, if I wanted to. Mom came into my room to say good night to me.

"Maybe we can have a dog," I said sleepily.

"It would be nice," Mom said, "but we won't be away that long."

That had been almost two years ago. My grandfather's hip and leg had been hurt a lot more than he'd known, or maybe admitted to himself at first, and the doctors doubted that he'd ever be able to manage his busy practice again. Mom's month of vacation ran out. She asked for an extended leave of absence from the New York clinic. And when Dad came home from the Antarctic trip, he and Mom and I spent an entire Sunday afternoon in the sunny living room of Grandfather's house, looking across the fields to the blue and purple mountains to the west while we talked. At the end of the afternoon, Mom and Dad called Grandfather in Florida and offered to buy the practice and stay in the valley.

All her friends in New York thought Mom had gone bananas, leaving a good job with a promising future at the clinic for the far rougher life of a farm vet. Mom just went on smiling her sweet smile, thanked everyone for their advice, and ignored every stitch of it. She and Dad and my grandfather were pleased, I was half out of my mind with delight, and we'd never for a moment been sorry since.

After Mom had taken over Grandfather's practice, a longtime client of his came to the house with a picnic basket and lifted out a seven-week-old puppy. It was coal black with a white ruff and four white paws and a streak of white like a chalk mark down its head. The puppy was handed to me, all leaks and wagging tail and small pink tongue.

"A welcome to the new doctor and her family," the man said. "No fancy pedigree papers, I'm afraid, but this pup's mother is mine, and she's one of the best dogs in the state. If you'd like him, he's yours."

So the puppy, Kim, was welcomed joyfully into our lives. The next new addition to our family was Rusty, a red-gold handsome chestnut horse outgrown by a neighbor's son who was going away to school. There was a small stable with two stalls near the house. It had been empty when we first came, though Grandad sometimes used it to take in a horse or a pony that needed special treatment for a few days at a time.

The horse's real name was October Gold, but everybody called him Rusty. He was mostly Quarter Horse, and Grandad knew him well. He told me so in reply to a delighted letter I'd written to tell him about Rusty's arrival.

"He's kind and gentle," Grandad wrote to me. "He'll be perfect for you, Kelly. You're lucky to have him."

Rusty was small, with four white socks and a blaze. I'd had some riding lessons, though mostly in a ring, so there was a lot I didn't know. I loved every minute of learning from Mom how to take care of him, and how to ride him in the pasture and around the farm until I felt brave enough to ride off our own place to neighboring farms and onto the lower paths on the mountains.

Through Rusty I was invited to 4-H Club meetings, and we held small shows, which were a lot of fun, every six weeks during the summer vacations. I made good friends, and we met to ride together on weekends whenever we could. We'd put sandwiches in our pockets and ride all day, with Kim skimming along beside us in the ripply, effortless run of his breed. I didn't miss the city for a minute and neither did Mom. Dad liked the farm, too. He hoped one day to be able to stay long enough to have a big garden and more animals, but he was still traveling a lot for his company. In the meantime, we let the neighbors hay our back fields in return for filling our hayloft, which meant plenty of good hay for Rusty and an occasional visiting patient of Mom's.

We always kept the spare stall ready. Rusty didn't mind visitors. And I knew the frightened foal would be happy to have Rusty in the next stall for company that night.

Chapter Four

Mom was very late getting home. I was in bed, but I wasn't asleep, and I saw the pattern of lights from her compact little truck move across my ceiling. When I heard the sound of the door opening and closing as she went into her office, I put on a bathrobe and went downstairs with Kim behind me.

"Hi," I said, poking my head in the door. "How's the Brewsters' Clydesdale?"

"Bad," Mom said in a discouraged voice. "And so is Lori's pony." She was reaching up to take a book from the shelf over her desk. "I've done everything I can for now. I hope the fever will be down by morning—it's terribly high."

She opened the book to look through the index. "Can I make you a sandwich and some coffee? Or tea?" I said.

Mom shook her head. She had found the page number she needed, and she sat down at her desk without taking her eyes from the book. "Thanks anyway, Kelly," she said in a faraway voice. "You go on back to bed. I'll be up soon."

I blew her a good-night kiss and went quietly back up the stairs to my room. She was obviously worried about Mr. Brewster's big horse, as well as Lori's pony, and it was late. I'd tell her about the foal I'd found on the mountain tomorrow.

Even though I was up early the next morning, Mom had already left. There was a note on the kitchen table for me. "I'll be at the Brewster farm first, if you need me. The telephone service will know where I am after that. Be home for lunch if I can. Love."

I was used to this. Farmers and vets got up before dawn a lot. I often didn't see Mom all day, but the friendly and efficient telephone answering service that covered most of the doctors and vets within miles always knew where Mom was—she let them know after each call—so I could always get in touch with her if I needed to. I let Kim out, had a huge bowl of cereal, and ate a handful of raisins as I went out to the stable.

I opened the door as quietly as I could, but the foal was frightened by the sound. I heard her throw herself against the stall wall in panic. I called out softly to her and to Rusty, who nickered in response, and the foal quieted down a little.

I didn't know what else to do to reassure her, so I went ahead with my usual stable chores with as little noise as possible. I gave Rusty and the foal a huge armful of fragrant hay first thing and then took time to look at the foal more carefully than I'd been able to do the evening before.

She was really a funny-looking little thing. Her muzzle was a mealy tan, with smudges of the same pale sandy tan under her eyes. Her coat was acorn brown with pale shadings of tan on her stomach and the top parts of her legs. There was a distinct black stripe down the center of her back, running from her scrubby black mane to the top of her short black tail. From the knees and hocks down, her legs were solid black. But above her knees and hocks, the black zebralike stripes on the pale tan background color looked like zig-zag zipper marks holding her together.

"That's what I'll call you," I said to the filly as I watched her eating her hay. "Zipper. Do you like the name?"

She put her ears back at me and twitched her short black tail crossly, but she went on eating hungrily.

"I've seen sweeter dispositions in my life," I said to her. "Don't be so cranky. Right now I'm the only friend you've got—other than Rusty, of course. And Kim. If it hadn't been for us, you'd have been dead as a doornail by now."

I wondered with amusement what was supposed to be so dead about a doornail as I gave Rusty his grain. Then I poured a generous measure of foal pellets into a rubber feed tub and went into the foal's stall.

Zipper put her ears back again, but she recognized the scent of the pellets. Watching me warily with her shiny black eyes, she came slowly over to me on stiff, hesitant little legs and dipped her tan muzzle into the tub.

I didn't put the tub down. I held it in my hands so the foal would have to get used to me and begin to understand that I was the bringer of good things to eat and meant her no harm.

She ate the white pellets quickly, chasing the last ones around the bottom of the tub with her strong lips. When she was sure there were none left, she sighed a little, almost contentedly, and went back to her hay.

She was thin. No wonder she was so hungry. If she'd been in the mountains with her straying mother all through the terribly stormy, cold spring, she must have had a hard first few months of life.

I filled the water buckets and went back to Zipper's stall. I stood just inside the door, letting her get used to me and wondering what to do next.

I was worried about what would happen if I turned her out in the pasture adjoining the stalls. She wasn't very big, but she was quick and very strong, and I was afraid she'd break right through the rail fence and run back up the mountain to look for her mother.

I didn't think she'd much like being in the stable alone, either, if I turned Rusty out without her. In the two years we'd been here in the valley, I'd ridden out with Mom on her calls a lot and had gotten a crash course on how violent a frightened or lonely or desperate horse could be. Even a young one, especially if it hadn't been handled much. Which this one clearly hadn't.

I cleaned Rusty's stall and gave him a thorough grooming. "You'll just have to babysit for one day," I told him with an apologetic pat on his shining neck. "It won't hurt you to stay in your stall for now to keep the foal company while I try to figure out what's best to do."

I opened the top of his outside door to let the sun and fresh air into his stall, but I left the foal's door closed and bolted. I'd seen an anxious foal go over the bottom half of a Dutch door once, when I was at another stable with Mom, and I felt pretty sure that Zipper would do the same thing. I didn't think it was worth the risk. I'd rescued her and brought her along this far—I didn't want to see the little foal ending up flat on the ground outside her half door with a broken neck. Not if I could help it.

I went to the tack room to call Lori. We were supposed to meet that afternoon for a ride, but I didn't want to take Rusty out and leave the foal alone in the stable, even if Rima was feeling better. I knew Lori would understand and we'd make plans for another day. But before I could dial the number, Mom called.

She sounded sad. The Brewsters' big horse had died. Less than an hour ago. And two others of the magnificent team had started to run fevers.

"I don't think I'll get back home all day," Mom said. "I've had calls from all over. I'm on my way to see two horses and a pony as quickly as I can—they don't sound good at all. Slight cough, high fever—Lori's pony has it, too. I don't know, Kelly. I wonder if they've got the same thing as the Brewsters' poor Clydesdale. The symptoms seem to be the same. . . ."

There wasn't much I could say, other than I was

sorry. I offered to come with her to help. I'd done this often, getting equipment and medicines from her unit for her as she needed them on calls—I knew which compartments held different things, where the vaccines were in the refrigerated sections, and how the hot water dispenser worked—and I liked helping. But Mom said no.

"Thanks anyway, but all the calls so far are from stables where there's enough help. You go for a nice ride and enjoy yourself. See you later."

She hung up, and I called Lori to sympathize about her pony. She sounded terribly worried.

We didn't talk for long. She wanted to go back to her sick pony and wait for Mom, who was coming again that morning to see Rima. I wished her good luck and said I'd call again that evening to hear how Rima was doing. I didn't tell Lori about the funny little foal I'd found on the mountain the day before; she had too much else to think about, I decided. But the real reason was that I didn't want anyone coming to the stable to see Zipper until the scared foal settled down more in her new surroundings.

Chapter Five

It was almost dark before Mom got home that evening. She looked exhausted. Her face was streaked with dust, and the crisp white coveralls she wore on her calls were limp and grimy. "Three of them," she said as she got stiffly out of her truck. "Three more cases today, just like Lori's pony and the Brewsters' Clydesdale. Don't come anywhere near me, Kelly, until I get out of these clothes. I don't know what we're dealing with here, but if it's some kind of an airborne virus that's making these horses so sick, I could be carrying it on my shoes and clothes. I've already changed four times into fresh coveralls. . . . I'll shower and change in the bathroom next to the office. Whatever these ponies and horses have got, it must be terribly contagious, and there's no way to tell yet how the disease is carried from one farm to another. Is Rusty all right?"

"He's fine," I said. "Bright and shining. Ate his supper like gangbusters."

"Good." Mom went into her office and I went to the kitchen to feed Kim and put the chops under the broiler for dinner.

After we'd finished, Mom poured herself a second cup of coffee and leaned back in her chair.

"Now tell me," she said. "What have you been up to these last two days?"

I grinned at her. "You're hardly going to believe this," I said, "but we've got a new horse. Well, almost a horse. It will be one day when it grows up."

I wasn't sure that anything would get Mom's mind off her sick patients but her polite interest turned into fascinated silence as I told her about finding the mare that had been killed by the fallen tree, and how I'd found her foal, Zipper, and brought her home.

"I wonder whom the mare belonged to," she said. "You'd think I'd have heard if one had run off and was lost. . . . How very strange. Maybe it was an Arabian or a Standardbred broodmare from one of the south valley breeding farms."

"Maybe," I said. "But I'd bet not. The mare killed by the fallen tree sure didn't look anything like any

Arabian I've ever seen. Or a Standardbred, either. From even the little I could see of the brown mare, she didn't look like *any* kind of horse I've ever seen before in my entire life."

Mom looked thoughtful. "Certainly *someone* must have heard of a lost horse, somewhere. It's not like losing track of a pet mouse or a rabbit. Horses are too big to go unnoticed, even if someone has a lot of them. That's why I wondered first about the big breeding farms, but those horses are worth a lot of money, and the farm managers keep a very careful eye on every one of them. . . ." Her voice trailed off in puzzled silence.

"Mom," I said. "This is the funniest-looking foal you ever saw. Believe me, it's not from any fancy breeding farm. Come see it. There's sure nobody around here that owns anything that even *begins* to look like Zipper."

"Perhaps the mare brought her foal across over the mountains," Mom suggested as I turned on the outside floodlights that lit the way to the stable. "And that's why you didn't recognize her."

"Maybe," I said. "But that's a pretty tough trip for a horse and a young foal, all that way, through that terrible winter we had, don't you think? You should see what a mess it is up there on the side of the mountain. Fallen rocks—some of them are huge.

Trees down all over, too. It looked as though whole pieces of the mountain fell apart last winter."

"It doesn't make sense any other way," said Mom, sounding definite.

"Okay." There was no use arguing with her when she spoke in that tone of voice.

"Let's go have a look," Mom said. We started to open the door just as the phone rang.

It was one of the vets at the clinic that took care of the horses at most of the big breeding farms in the lower part of the valley.

"Yes," I heard Mom say. "I've got three new cases and I lost one just this morning. . . . That's right, slight cough, very high fever. There's not a one that's responding to any of the usual courses of treatment —I couldn't even bring the fever down on the horse that just died. It looked something like encephalitis, but every one of the sick horses and ponies I've worked with so far has been fully inoculated. I was going to call you this evening to ask if you'd had anything like this in your part of the valley. . . ."

Mom drew her breath in sharply. "Five? And you've lost one other. . . . Yes, I sent blood and tissue samples out this morning to two labs. Have you gotten preliminary reports back from any lab yet?

"Nothing." Mom tapped a pencil against her teeth and frowned at the phone. "This certainly doesn't look good. If it's a virus, it's not exactly like any I've ever seen, and there were some pretty strange outbreaks at the racetracks in the East during the years I was there. Horses coming in from all parts of the world, even after quarantine. . . . Bacterial? I suppose it could be, but it doesn't respond to any of the antibiotics I've used. . . . Yes, of course I think we should keep in close touch. We may well have the beginning of an epidemic on our hands and we don't have the faintest clue as to what it might be. Yes. This certainly should be reported to the state veterinarian. First thing tomorrow morning."

Mom hung up the phone slowly and put the pencil down on the table. "Strange business," she said. "Well." She straightened her shoulders. "Let's have a look at this new creature of yours, Kelly. And then I'm going to make a few more calls."

"The foal's kind of wild and spooky," I said as we walked together toward the stable.

"Of course." Mom nodded.

"I've been giving her Foalac pellets and hay," I said. "I don't know if she's old enough to handle regular grain yet. I can't tell. I figured she'd do well enough on the pellets until I could ask you."

Zipper and Rusty were both lying down when we went into the stable and turned on the lights. Rusty didn't bother to get up, but we could hear the foal jumping to her feet right away.

"She bites," I warned Mom. "And she kicks, too. Hard."

Mom smiled. "It sounds as though you've got a real tiger in there. I can't wait to meet her."

Zipper bounced off the oak walls of her stall once or twice in fright when we stopped at her door. "Wait just a minute," I said to Mom. "I'll get a treat for her."

Zipper recognized the black feed tub right away when I carried it into her stall. She watched Mom suspiciously, but she ate the handful of pellets I'd put in the tub.

"She's a whole lot better behaved already," I said to Mom, speaking quietly. "Look. I can even touch her neck now. . . ."

Mom hadn't said a word. I glanced over at her and was astounded to see the look of shock on her face.

"What's the matter?" I asked uneasily. "Do you recognize the foal after all? Do you know where she came from?"

"In a way," said Mom in a funny voice. She didn't say another word. She watched Zipper in silence as the foal finished the feed and stood quietly, for a change, under the light in the stall.

I stroked her neck and ran my hand down her

short black mane. "This is real progress," I said proudly. "Things will go even better when I can manage to get a halter on her. . . ."

Mom still didn't say anything. I gave Rusty and the foal a little more hay, said good night to them, turned off the lights, and closed the stable door.

Chapter Six

"How old do you think Zipper is?" I asked Mom as we went back to the house.

"Five months, I'd guess. Possibly six. Though I can't be absolutely sure without looking at her teeth," Mom said. She still sounded distracted.

"She's got lots of those. For sure," I said, making a face as I rubbed my arm, remembering the bites the foal had given me the day before. My arms had several black-and-blue marks, just as my shins did from the sharp kicks that had reached me while I was untangling the angry, frightened foal from the vines.

Kim followed us as Mom led the way to her office. She turned on the lights and sat down on the couch with a single volume of the encyclopedia in her hands. I was mystified. Mom put the book down on the table in front of us and turned to the page she was looking for. "Just look at this, Kelly," Mom said.

"What's a picture of Zipper doing in an encyclopedia?" I said, staring in amazement at the photographs in the book. The pictures were of Zipper, or a lot of little horses just like her, jumping around in paintings done on a background that looked like stone. "Almost every one of them looks like Zipper—the shading, the stripes, everything. What in the world . . . ?" Puzzled, I finally thought to look at the captions under the pictures.

"Cave paintings in France?" I said. "And in Spain—from the Ice Age? Mom, that's over ten thousand years ago. It says so, right here. What on earth . . . ?"

"Here's more." Mom handed me another book. There was a color photograph of Zipper on the cover. "Look inside," Mom said, sitting down beside me. Page after page showed little shaded dun horses standing, running, or jumping in the air, frozen in time by Ice Age art. And nearly every one of them could have been a glowing, living portrait of Zipper.

There was a long silence. "Whatever is Zipper doing in these books?" I said finally.

"I think a better question would be what she's doing in our own stable," said Mom. "These are all pictures of *prehistoric* horses. These are all Ice Age cave paintings, Kelly. Beautiful, aren't they? Beautiful."

I turned the pages of the book slowly. "Prehistoric horses," I repeated slowly. "But true wild horses have been extinct in this country for thousands and thousands of years. There aren't any left in the Americas. All of them vanished—we learned that in school. And they're supposed to be extinct now all over the world."

"Maybe so," said Mom in a low voice. "But look at these cave paintings. Not just at the markings on the horses, but the unusual shape of the heads. The big cheekbones, the way the eyes are placed, the set of the ears. And the tails—black, set low on the hindquarters. It's all just like Zipper. I wish I could have seen the adult mare you found. Could you see anything more than the head? Was her mane short and black?"

I nodded. I had no trouble picturing in my mind the look of the horse trapped under the tree. She'd had the very short black forelock and the same distinctively shaped head as those in the paintings in the books on the table in front of me.

I described her again to Mom.

"You're just going to have to take my word for it, I guess," I said. "But this is exactly the same horse.

I *told* you she looked different from any horse I'd ever seen before."

Mom nodded in silence. I turned the pages of the books with my mind spinning. "Look," I said suddenly. "Here's a photograph and a drawing of two little carvings—they're in museums in Europe, and the book says they're from the Ice Age, too."

Mom looked at the photograph and smiled, almost numbly. "I know," she said. "And they could have been done yesterday. Each one is an exact portrait of your new wild filly."

"This is crazy," I said. "We can't have an extinct foal in our barn. It doesn't make any sense at all."

"I think we'd better think this through for a little while, before we tell anyone about your Zipper," Mom said at last. "Or even let anyone else see her. There must be a sensible answer to this. We're just not thinking clearly enough. I feel as though we must be hallucinating. She's got to be some kind of a throwback, probably to some horses that ran off years ago and nobody cared. Or perhaps some mustangs came across the mountains from far away, driven by those terrible storms. Mustangs aren't true wild horses, of course, nice as it is to have them out there. There weren't horses of any kind in the Americas after the prehistoric horse vanished. Not until Cortez brought a few over from Spain to Mexico in the early 1500s. . . ."

The phone rang and Mom reached out to answer it. "Right," she said. "I'm on my way." She stood up. "It's Mark's gray horse, Pennant," she said. "He's running a high fever—" She pressed her hand against her tired eyes for a moment.

"Too much," she said, giving her short, curly hair a brisk shake. "Didn't you go for a ride with Mark this afternoon?"

"I didn't go," I said. "It got too complicated. I was afraid to take Rusty out and leave Zipper alone. But I talked to Mark, and he didn't say Pennant was sick."

"This fever hits hard, and suddenly, in the cases I've seen so far," Mom said grimly. "I think we're into real trouble with this disease, whatever it is. And we don't even know how it spreads. Kelly, don't ride with anyone until we get a handle on this. Keep Rusty away from other horses." Mom sighed. "I hope I can help Pennant."

Mark's nice gray horse, Pennant, was still alive—I called the next day to make sure. Mark was half out of his mind with worry. Mom had been to his place twice that morning and was coming again in the afternoon. I talked to Lori, too, of course, but Mom believed Rima was dying in spite of all that had been done for the pony.

I didn't know if Lori knew this. She didn't say

so and I didn't either, but I felt the sorrow behind Lori's words. She knew, all right, somehow, though she didn't want to admit it and give up hope.

I fussed around my own stable, grooming Rusty until he began to fidget with impatience. I fed Zipper a handful of pellets several times, and stroked her neck and spoke to her softly and constantly. I tried to get a small halter on her, too, but there was no way she was going to let me buckle it on her head. She shied away violently whenever I tried, no matter how carefully and slowly I moved, and she was far too strong for me to force her to stand still to accept it.

Chapter Seven

It was a shimmery sunny day, with a bright breeze blowing. I knew it wasn't good for Rusty to stay in his stall indefinitely. I'd been planning to ask Mom if she knew of someone who would lend us a pony to keep Zipper company in the stable while I turned Rusty out, or went for a ride, but the frightening new sickness had put a stop to that idea.

I went outside and sat with Kim in the shade of a tree. "We've got a real problem," I said to the dog. "I know the foal will come apart at the seams if she's left alone in the stable, but it isn't fair to Rusty to keep him shut up this way. And it's not good for the filly, either."

Kim flopped over on his back and waved his paws in the air, inviting me to rub his stomach.

"I can't tell," I said to the dog, "whether I'm

being selfish or sensible. I don't want Zipper to run back onto the mountain. I don't want to lose her, and I really don't think she'd survive there more than a night or two. She'd be alone and defenseless, searching for her poor mother, and there are bears and wildcats up there. . . . Anyway, it's fun having her here, and I want to keep her and tame her, whatever she is."

Kim licked my hand. He was a wonderful listener.

"But I can't keep her and Rusty locked up forever, like lions in a cage in some kind of rotten zoo," I said, making up my mind at last. "She's got to go out of her stall some time. Come on, Kim, let's check the fencing to make sure all the rails are up. And then I'm going to turn Rusty and Zipper out together in the pasture."

Kim and I walked every inch of the pasture fence. I jiggled each rail that looked the least bit loose and jammed it more firmly into its post. I checked the latches on the two wide gates and then shook them to make sure they were tight.

"Okay, Kim," I said at last. "I can't put this off any longer." I went to the stable and, before I could change my mind, slid the bolts back and opened the outside doors of the stalls.

Rusty came out of his stall like a bombshell, running and bucking with joy across the soft grass.

Zipper hurled herself along beside him in a bobbing, short-strided gallop, swinging her head from side to side, bewildered by her sudden freedom.

They charged across the pasture, and I could hardly bear to watch as they neared the fence line. The rails looked more and more frail and thin, the closer they got to them, and I knew very well that the foal, small though she was, could throw herself against them and break through if she really wanted to go.

Rusty turned and galloped back toward the stable. Zipper skidded in an uneven circle and stopped. She whinnied once, and the echo bounced back at her from the mountain. She listened, standing motionless beside the fence. And then she turned and galloped back across the field to Rusty.

I slumped against the stable door and caught my breath in a gasp of relief. The first challenge was over. I'd gambled on horses hating to be alone if they could have company. Clearly the foal was old enough to be weaned, and so she didn't have the frantic pull to get back to look for her mother. Within a few minutes Rusty had rolled luxuriously in his favorite spot, covering his freshly groomed coat with dust and grass, and settled down to graze contentedly.

Zipper watched with curiosity, skipped to the

side, and then she, too, started nibbling quietly at the tips of the pasture grass.

Dr. Marshall, the state veterinarian, came that afternoon. The next day the federal emergency disease task force came all the way from Maryland. Every farm in the valley was quarantined. There was a strict ban on any horses coming in or out of the valley.

"All we can do right now is try to contain this, and eradicate it here if we can," Dr. Marshall said to Mom. "Let's hope it won't be long before we identify the cause and find a treatment that works —and while we're at it, let's hope this disease doesn't spread beyond the valley."

I hardly saw Mom at all through the next two weeks. I felt quarantined along with the horses—no one came riding over to see me, of course, but this was just as well, since I wanted Zipper to settle down a lot more before she saw another horse. Mark's Pennant had died two days after he first got sick, and Rima had died the day before. There'd been three doctors working over them—Mom had called for outside opinions—but no one had been able to help either the lovely pony or the horse.

I wished I could drive, so that Mom could at least have a rest going from farm to farm, but I couldn't.

I did all kinds of things at home to make things as easy as I could for her, like weeding her small vegetable garden. I didn't mind doing this at all. I loved the warm scent of the tomato plants in the sunlight, the bright orange knobs of the carrots under their feathery tops, and the scarlet glow of the beets just beginning to show above the soft earth. I rode Rusty inside the pasture, practicing figure eights at a trot and a canter for the next 4-H show, though I knew it would probably be cancelled. Zipper bopped along beside Rusty every step of the way.

We had a big freezer, well stocked with food, and I rode my bike to the small general store a little more than a mile down the road for fresh milk and fruit. I usually did these errands for Mom on Rusty, carrying the groceries home in big saddlebags, and it had been fun, but I had to settle for the bike for now.

Most of all, I tried not to worry about the dreadful sickness that was spreading every day.

Mom was so tired her eyes burned in her face and were ringed with dark shadows. Mr. and Mrs. Brewster brought her home in their pickup truck early one afternoon.

"The last of our Clydesdales just died," Mrs. Brewster told me as she helped Mom into the house. "I guess it was the last straw for your mother—she loved them as much as we did. We all kept hoping for a miracle, but it never happened. Persuade your mother to go to bed, Kelly, if you possibly can, and call the doctor. Maybe he can convince her there's no use in killing herself trying to save everyone's horses. She's a very fine vet, but even she can't do the impossible. There's not a thing *any* of the vets can do."

In spite of Mom's protests, I did exactly that. I coaxed her to bed and called the doctor. When he came he gave Mom a lecture and a shot, and told her not to move out of bed for two solid days.

The doctor and I talked a few minutes outside the front door. "You're pretty young for all this responsibility," he said. "Are you sure you can manage? I can find a housekeeper to lend you a hand if you need one. Mrs. Henderson helped take care of your grandfather before he went to Florida, and I'm sure she'd be glad to come—"

"Thank you," I said. "But Mom's not sick, is she? Just worn out. I can get pretty bossy if I have to, believe me. I'll make her stay in bed, somehow, and I can manage the house and farm. There's not that much to do, and I can call you if I need you, can't I? And Mrs. Brewster said she'd come by or call in the morning. I'm okay."

The doctor nodded. "All right, but I'd like to

hear from you tomorrow. Do what you can to persuade your mother to take it easy for a little while. I can understand how she feels—she's tired and angry and frustrated. She feels so helpless, of course. So do the other vets. All their training, and all their skills, and all the new drugs available today, and not a bit of it worth a thing when one of these new viruses shows up. . . . I remember working through an epidemic of diphtheria some years back. Terrible . . . and at least we knew what it was. . . ."

He patted my shoulder and drove away. I went back to Mom's room. She was sound asleep. I unplugged the phone beside her bed and tiptoed out of the room.

Chapter Eight

Mark called. I sympathized awkwardly with him over the loss of Pennant, feeling a little bit guilty that Rusty and the foal were still so bright and well. Not that I'd told him yet, or anyone else, about Zipper. It didn't matter, anyway, with the gloom hanging over the valley. And in spite of everything that had been done, the virus was spreading.

I turned the television set on to keep me company just in time to hear a news report. A few racetracks in different parts of the country had been closed—due, the announcer said, to a minor outbreak of a new coughing virus. The tracks were expected to open again in a few days.

"Ha," I said back to the announcer. "That's what *you* think." There'd been a few little pieces on the sports pages of the newspapers within the last few days. This horse and that wouldn't be racing as expected. "Running a slight fever" was the excuse they used. There'd been no major stories about the new sickness yet. I wondered sadly how many horses had already died, and how long the tracks and breeders would try to keep it a secret.

I couldn't understand the silence. Surely the tracks and trainers knew of the terrible outbreak of the unidentified virus, even if most of the cases were still confined to our valley. It was unreasonable to expect or even dare hope it wouldn't spread further. It was a threat hanging over every single horse in the country. . . . Did the rest of the world know? Didn't anybody care?

"Of course they know," Mom explained that evening. "The silence about all this is because of money. Megabucks, Kelly. Billions involved in racehorses. Imports and exports, big investment money in buying and selling. They don't want any kind of frightening publicity. It makes investors nervous. But the silence in the media won't last much longer. The federal agency is planning a very strict quarantine, not only in our valley, but also for the entire country, until we get this under some kind of control. So many horses are flown overseas today . . . every day . . . and it would take only one infected horse to introduce the sickness into another country."

Two more of my friends called. They were feeling as trapped as I was with their horses, and just as afraid. The 4-H show had been cancelled as I'd expected, and everybody was keeping the horses and ponies at home and hoping for the best.

I even tried to call Dad just to hear his comforting voice. He was back in the Antarctic. Whenever he was away he called us at least once a week, and through radio phones he usually could be reached. But the operator said they were having a severe storm and had temporarily lost radio contact, so that was the end of that good idea.

I gave up and went out to bring Rusty and Zipper into the stable for the night.

Rusty was grazing quietly while the foal raced in circles around him. She never seemed to tire. When Rusty wouldn't join her in her mad gallops, she chased after butterflies and birds, though she never went far from his side.

As I watched her, I thought again of the books Mom had showed me. How could Zipper possibly be a true wild horse if there weren't any left? "Extinct" was such a definite word. It didn't leave much room for argument. But there sure was nothing extinct about Zipper.

I heard Rusty cough, just once, as I went to rinse

out and refill his water bucket. I froze with the handle of the bucket clenched in my hand. I couldn't even breathe. But he didn't cough again.

"He must have had a scrap of grass caught in his throat," I said to Kim, and went on with my chores. Zipper was bouncing in her stall with impatience for her feed. Mom had said it would be all right to mix a handful of crushed oats with her pellets, and she loved them. Rusty nickered for his feed, but he didn't plunge his muzzle into the grain as he usually did.

"You stuffed yourself with too much grass in the pasture all day," I told him. I watched him carefully for a while. Eventually he did start to nibble at his grain. I leaned on his stall door, looking at him uneasily, but he seemed okay to me.

"Too much good pasture grass," I repeated to Kim as we went back to the house. "He's just not as hungry as usual, that's all." But it was impossible to still the small, dark feeling of dread I'd felt since I'd heard Rusty's one short cough.

"I'm witch hunting," I said crossly to poor Kim, who thought I was scolding him. "I'm finding ghosts and goblins and awful things just because I'm scared." I reassured the worried dog as well as I could, gave him his supper, and busied myself scrambling some eggs for Mom and me.

She was awake and smiled at me as I knocked and came into her room.

"I feel better already," she said. "All I needed was a little sleep."

"Sure," I said lightly. "But the doctor said you're to stay in bed for two days. Like it or not."

Mom sighed and put her head back on the pillows. "I guess he's right," she said. "The poor Brewsters—they were so kind. Losing the last of those lovely, lovely horses and then having me come apart in their stable . . . ."

I'd brought both our suppers on a tray. Mom and I chatted about everything in the world except horses as we ate. I made her a fresh cup of hot tea, but by the time I went back upstairs with the steaming cup, she was fast asleep again.

Kim and I watched television together in the living room after the few dishes were done. I drank the tea I'd made for Mom. One of the doctors from the clinic called, and I answered the phone.

"There's an expert in animal epidemics coming to our clinic late tomorrow afternoon, for a conference," he said. "We thought your mother might like to meet him."

I thanked him and told him about Mom's collapsing that afternoon.

"I know," he said. "I'm sorry. She called to ask if we'd cover for her the next two days, and of course we'll be glad to. Tell her not to worry. All of us are doing the best we can. I just wish we could do more."

"I'll give her your message when she wakes up," I promised. "I know the doctor said she should stay in bed, but I'm sure she'll want to come anyway, if she possibly can."

I went out to the stable again to look at Rusty. He hadn't finished all his grain, but he was eating some hay.

"You're all right," I told him fiercely. He came to the stall door and pressed his muzzle gently against my cheek.

Zipper had discovered that if she put her forehoofs on the sill, she was tall enough to look over her stall door. She watched with her strange, almond-shaped dark eyes glittering in the stable lights and her black-rimmed, sandy ears pricked with interest. I went to give her a pat and a piece of a carrot before I said good night, turned off the lights, and went back to the house.

Chapter Nine

I woke up just after dawn had broken the next morning. I could hear birds making happy morning sounds in the tree outside my bedroom window, and the first patterns of early sunlight brightened my windowsill.

Mom was still asleep. I slipped into a pair of fresh jeans and a sweatshirt—the morning was cool—found my sneakers and a pair of socks under my bed, and tiptoed down the stairs.

Kim greeted me with joy and went out with me into the new morning. There were lacy patterns of cobwebs on the grass, and a haze of mist covered the lower land between the pasture and the stream. The pale-green willows raised their graceful branches to curve back into the silver mist hiding the silent stream below.

Dreamily, and still half-asleep, I opened the stable door.

The peace of the summer morning shattered like broken icicles around me as I looked into Rusty's stall to say good morning to him. He was standing motionless in the center of his stall with his head down and his legs spread. His usually shining red-gold coat was dry and harsh. I didn't need to be a vet to know he was a very sick horse.

I clutched at the top of his stall door. I didn't want to believe what I was seeing. "Rusty?" I said in a shaking voice. He barely turned his head to look at me with sad, dull eyes.

I made myself let go of the door, sucked in a deep breath, and went to look at Zipper. She was as bright as ever, coming quickly to the door to see if I'd brought her breakfast.

I poured pellets and a half measure of crushed oats into her feed tub and, for the first time, did no more than put it on the floor inside her door. I threw her an armful of hay and hurried to look at Rusty again.

His water bucket was empty. I filled it to the brim and held it near him so he needn't move if he were thirsty and wanted a drink. He took a few sips and lowered his head again.

I felt his ears, which were incredibly cold, and ran my hand down his neck—his skin felt hot and tight and his coat was dry and standing on end. I didn't need a thermometer to tell me that he was running a very high fever.

In spite of our quarantine, Rusty clearly had whatever it was that was killing all the horses.

I didn't know what to do. There was no use in waking poor Mom. She'd seen enough cases and so had every other vet I could think of, and there wasn't a single horse they'd been able to help, in any way, no matter how hard they'd tried.

I ran outside the stable for no reason at all. The hardest thing in the world to do was nothing, and there was nothing to be done. Maybe, when Mom woke up, she could tell me, at least, how I might make poor Rusty more comfortable—I found it impossible to believe we had to wait and watch my horse die by inches. Even when I knew better.

I went back into the house, tripping clumsily over the doorsill to the kitchen. I supposed I should have some breakfast, but I sure wasn't hungry. I wandered around the familiar room, bumping into the table. I gave Kim a dog biscuit to give myself something to do. I turned on the radio. Nothing but livestock reports. At least the killing disease was limited only to horses. The cattle market was booming, there was a growing interest in sheep—who cared, with poor Rusty so sick? I was reaching to change the station when an interview started with an expert on animal epidemics.

"Tell us, Doctor," the interviewer said. "Why is there talk of quarantine on all the horses in our country? Not much has been reported in the media so far about this. Can you clarify what we're dealing with?"

"There's been an outbreak of an unknown virus in horses that we can't control," the epidemiologist said bluntly. "It's highly contagious, it is spreading rapidly, and until we find a way to stop it, it is a threat to horses and ponies everywhere. A federal quarantine will keep this lethal virus from possibly spreading worldwide."

"So there it is." Mom, wrapped in her bathrobe, had come to the kitchen door. "At last. They're admitting publicly what so many of us have known for so long." She stopped to listen, but the short interview had ended in a noisy commercial. I switched off the radio.

Mom went to fill the teakettle and put it on the stove. "There's got to be a source. There's got to be a reason." She took a container of orange juice from the refrigerator, poured herself a glassful, and sat down at the kitchen table.

Even though she looked terribly worried, she

looked a little more rested and fresh than she had in weeks. I offered to make breakfast and take it up to her room for her, but she shook her head firmly.

"I couldn't stay flat in bed another minute," she said. "It won't hurt for me just to poke around the house a little bit. You don't have to fuss over me any more, Kelly, though you've been wonderful."

I stared unseeingly out of the kitchen window. "Kelly," Mom said gently. "There's something the matter. I can tell. What is it?"

"You're supposed to be resting," I said crisply. "And no worries. For at least another day."

Mom got up and came over to put her arms around me. "Tell me, Kelly. Did Zipper get out and run away during the night?"

I shook my head, not trusting myself to speak.

"Rusty." Mom went back to the table and sat down to stare at the bubbles in her orange juice glass. "He's sick, isn't he? And the filly, too?"

"Zipper's fine," I said, speaking carefully. "Bright as a new penny."

"Then it *is* Rusty." Mom turned her glass with the tips of her fingers. "Fever? Maybe a little cough?"

"That's right." I turned to face her. "He looks terrible, Mom. And it's so awful, knowing there's nothing, nothing, *nothing* we can do."

"It's so hard to believe. I keep hoping it's all a

bad dream and I'll wake up and it will be over."

Mom stood up and went upstairs. In a few minutes she was down again in jeans, with her hair tied back with a blue bandanna. "I've got to see him, Kelly."

Wordlessly we went together to the stable. I heard Mom take a sharp breath when she saw Rusty. "Ice," she said to me. "There's a lot of it in the freezer. Bring some as quickly as you can."

I didn't stop to ask any questions. I brought the ice. Mom already had managed to help Rusty outside and was turning on the hose. "The fever is so high it weakens the horses and kills them before their systems have any chance to develop antibodies to fight off this sickness. Wrap a lot of cubes in a grooming towel and rub it over Rusty's head. And we'll get cool water on him—anything that might help to bring the fever down a little. What these poor horses need is time."

Rusty looked sicker than ever out in the bright daylight. Numbly I did what Mom had said while she ran the water from the hose over the unprotesting horse. He didn't even bother to try to shake it off.

"He's not dead yet," Mom said in a low voice. "I can't, I won't, just sit in the house and wait for him to die. Can you hold the hose on him for a few minutes, as well as the ice? I'll try some of the medications I've got—not that they've been of any use so far, but I hate to give up hope completely—"

She ran to the office. I knew how she felt. Doing something, anything, would make us feel a fraction less defeated. At least we were fighting back in every way we could.

Mom took blood samples from Rusty and then gave him three different injections. "These aren't cures," she said. "I'm just giving him everything I can think of to try to bring his fever down."

I offered Rusty some fresh clover I'd picked; it was one of his favorite treats. He wouldn't even take it into his mouth. I let the clover spill to the ground from my hand.

"We're missing something," Mom said, almost angrily. "The labs have tested all the blood and tissue samples from the horses that died. And they haven't found a clue. Maybe we've been waiting too long to take the blood samples. Rusty's only been sick a few hours, from everything you've told me, and you know the horse well. Even a few hours might make a difference. Worth a try, anyway. I'll send Rusty's blood samples to a small virology lab I know. The doctor who runs it is a real Sherlock Holmes and he uses his own research systems. I know he'll be interested. . . ." Her voice trailed off.

She took the blood samples to her office refrigerator, and when she came back, Zipper was whinnying pitifully from her stall. "She's looking for Rusty," I said. "She'll start pounding the wall with her forehoofs in a minute. She doesn't like to be alone."

Sure enough, in a few moments, we heard Zipper strike the oak planks of her stall sharply with one hoof. I knew from experience that this was only the beginning.

"She certainly sounds as though she feels perfectly well," Mom said in a murmur, half to herself. "That's an unusual break. Generally, when horses have been stabled so closely together, they've gotten sick within hours of each other."

"She's eating up a storm," I said. "She hasn't shown a single sign of feeling sick."

Mom went on running cool water over Rusty and looked around the stable yard. "If you shut the big gate to the drive, I think you could turn her loose out here perfectly safely. She's going to hurt herself, striking at the stall walls the way she's doing, and we don't need that on top of everything else. And there's no use worrying about her getting close to Rusty. Since she's been stabled right beside him, she's already been thoroughly exposed to what he's got."

I ran to do as Mom suggested and let Zipper out

of her stall. She trotted quickly down the aisle and out the open door and settled down to start grazing peacefully in the stable yard.

The sun rose higher. Zipper came over to inspect the hose, pulled at it with her teeth, and played with the water as it spilled off Rusty's back.

"She looks marvelous, doesn't she?" Mom said, watching the filly. "She's put on weight and lost that ribby look she had. And, what's more important, she looks the picture of health. Her eyes are bright, and she's alert—she doesn't look sick at all."

Chapter Ten

Mom suddenly stopped talking, and her eyes got a faraway look.

"Tell me again about the day you found her," she said. "Right from the very beginning."

I was glad to have something to think of other than how awful Rusty looked and how terribly sick he was. I described the whole morning's ride I'd taken on Rusty, the huge boulders that had been tumbled onto the bridle path by the past winter's savage storms, and the wide crack in the sheer stone ledge where snow or ice might have broken through during the storms or in the sudden spring thaw.

"I think that's what must have loosened the roots of the tree that fell on Zipper's dam, wherever she came from," I said. "There were a lot of enormous fallen rocks and heaps of fallen trees from the crack in the mountain. All together."

Mom listened in concentrated silence. "I've had a totally crazy idea," she said finally. "But that doesn't matter, because the dying horses have driven us all a bit crazy. A little more won't hurt. If I'm right, though, we might be able to save Rusty, after all."

"I don't believe it," I said in a flat voice. "You're only trying to make me feel better. What can my story about finding Zipper do to help poor Rusty?"

I glanced at Mom. Maybe she was getting hysterical from all the strain she'd been through. But she sure didn't look hysterical; she looked thoughtful. And enormously determined.

"We've been working with something we know nothing about. Neither does anyone else. I don't know if I'm right about Zipper . . . but suppose, just suppose for a minute, she is a true wild horse. A tarpan, or Przewalski, or Mongolian wild horse—whatever people may call them today—looking just the same as the little horses in the Ice Age Paintings.

"There are several herds of small dun horses in captivity in zoos and wildlife preserves in different parts of the world that are believed to be the last of the true ancient wild horses. A Russian explorer, Przewalski, caught a few in the late 1800s in northern Asia. More were captured later. The Bronx zoo has imported some, and San Diego, and a couple of other zoos in this country. Almost every one of these horses is a sandy shaded dun, with black markings and a short, upright mane. Like the horses in the Ice Age paintings and carvings. Like Zipper."

Mom took a deep breath. "Kelly, if I *am* right about Zipper, she might be from a genuine Ice Age wild herd that survived in *this* country somehow, living through whatever wiped out the rest of the horses throughout the Americas. A few horses *could* have stayed hidden safely away in isolated spots in the mountains for generation after generation, living, breeding, and dying far away from people or other horses. And possibly they were able to develop immune systems, thousands of years ago, that could fight off viral infections our horses of today can't handle.

"Why not? There are several theories, but it *might* have been a virus that was responsible for destroying the ancient herds of horses on the American continents. And I mean all the way through Canada right down to the tip of South America."

"Mom," I said cautiously, "you're talking like a second-rate science fiction movie."

She wasn't listening. "If this is true, and Zipper is from a hidden Ice Age herd, with the right kind of immunity, she could be carrying antibodies in her blood to fight this miserable virus."

I stared speechlessly at Mom. "So that would be

great for Zipper," I said after a few moments. "She sure looks well enough. But how can she help Rusty?"

"Antibodies," Mom said again. "To help *him* fight the virus."

"How can you tell?" I said, almost wildly. "Rusty's dying. I know that as well as you do, even if you haven't said so. There's no time for labs to find special antibodies, even if Zipper does have them."

"She either has them or she doesn't," said Mom. "Serum from her blood can't do any harm to Rusty. We have nothing to lose by trying."

Mom handed me the hose. "I've got to draw some blood from Zipper," she said.

Confused as I was, I had to laugh. "Mom, she's getting much tamer. Every day. But I still can't get a halter on her, no matter how I try. She can't tolerate any kind of confinement except in her stall, and she sure doesn't like that very much, either. How do you expect her to stand still for you to take any blood from her?"

"There are ways, if it matters enough," Mom said. "And this matters. Keep the water running over Rusty. I'm going to get some supplies from the office."

She wouldn't say anything more. I did as I was

told, moving the stream of water from Rusty's head all down his back and under his stomach without stopping. The gravel outside the barn was full of puddles by now. I sloshed around in them, not caring.

Mom came back with a jar of white powder. "You've said that Zipper's a greedy little thing," she said. "What exactly have you been feeding her? What does she like best?"

I told her, and she went to make up a mixture of pellets and oats. She brought the feed tub outside and measured several spoonfuls of the powder over the top of the grain.

"Here," she said, giving the tub to me. "Zipper is used to you feeding her. Give her this."

I handed her the hose and took the rubber tub over near the fence where Zipper was grazing. I didn't ask any questions. Zipper saw the feed tub in my hands and came trotting over to me with her funny little ears pricked and her black eyes gleaming with interest. She snorted at the strange white powder, wiggled it around in the grain with her upper lip, and began to eat happily.

"There," I said when the tub was empty. "She ate it all. Now what?"

"Now we wait," said Mom in a tense voice. Zipper pushed at my hands gently with her soft tan muzzle to make sure I didn't have anything more to give her, then trotted off to graze again.

About twenty minutes later, she yawned, shook her head lazily, and poked without much interest at a fresh patch of grass.

"She's getting sick, too," I said, looking frantically at Mom. But Mom just smiled. It was the first time I'd seen her smile for a long time.

"Don't worry," she said. "Honestly. She's just getting sleepy. That powder I gave her was a tranquilizer. A strong one."

Five minutes later, Zipper was flat on the ground, sound asleep.

"It worked," said Mom. "Now for the next step."

In a short time, Mom had a vial of Zipper's dark-red blood in her hand.

Holding it carefully, she hurried to her office, and I heard the whir of her centrifuge through the open window.

It wasn't long before she was back, carrying a vial of pale-yellow liquid. It looked like nothing more than plain, slightly discolored tap water.

"Serum," Mom said. "I spun the serum from Zipper's blood in the centrifuge. It may not be standard medical procedure, Kelly, but you might keep your fingers crossed."

Rusty stood absolutely motionless, not caring, as

Mom slowly injected the serum into the big vein in his neck.

The hours passed. There was nothing more to do but wait and hope, if we dared. Zipper woke up, got to her feet, stretched like a cat, and started to graze again as though nothing had happened.

Rusty, soaking in the running water, didn't notice a thing that went on around him. I'd suggested to Mom that she go into the house to lie down for a little while in the middle of the day, but she was back out in less than an hour with a plate of sandwiches and two glasses of milk.

At least I was able to persuade her to sit on the bench at the stable door while I held Rusty and she and I both ate our sandwiches. I never knew what was in mine. I couldn't have tasted anything, but I managed to choke them down.

"*If* Zipper does have antibodies against this virus, it may be several hours before there are any signs of their helping Rusty," Mom said. "Waiting's always the hardest part, isn't it?"

I just nodded.

The sun dipped behind the hills, and a cool breeze blew across the pasture. Zipper came over to me and nudged me with her muzzle. I looked at my watch. No wonder—it was time for her regular evening feed, and Zipper always knew. She followed me into the stable and I fed her, leaving her feed tub on the floor and the stall door open so she could come back to Rusty when she had finished.

I couldn't imagine exactly what we were waiting for. A sudden, blazing magic cure, I thought to myself, a little bitterly, but I didn't want to say so. Mom looked so hopeful. We went on pouring cool water over the feverish horse. Nothing changed.

It was starting to get dark when Rusty raised his head. He turned it and pressed it against Mom's shoulder. I watched, hardly daring to believe what I was seeing, as he nuzzled the sleeve of her soaked shirt in his familiar sweet manner.

"Get him some water," Mom said. I flew to get his bucket. I filled it with fresh water from the hose, and Rusty lowered his head to drink, swishing the surface playfully with his muzzle as he'd so often done before, when he was well.

"He's better," I whispered.

"He is," said Mom.

Chapter Eleven

The next few hours went by in a blur. I still didn't ask any questions. There'd be time enough for that later on. All that mattered was that Rusty followed me back to his stall with his head up, and walking with a steady, sure stride.

"He'll be tired after all this," said Mom, smiling as though she couldn't stop. "Give him a nice bran mash, if he'll eat anything. Are there any new carrots in the garden? They'd be good. I'll get some."

I mixed a warm bran mash with a handful of crushed oats in it while Mom cut up the small carrots she'd brought from the garden. I stirred them into the mash. Mom and I stood and watched the horse eat almost all of it and turn to nibble at his hay.

"I don't believe it," I said at last.

Mom and I hugged each other speechlessly.

When everything was put away, and Zipper and Rusty were comfortable in their stalls, Mom and I folded like weary balloons in the living room. Mom was stretched out on the couch with her hands folded behind her head; I was curled up in my favorite big armchair next to the fireplace.

"I suppose you know I hardly understand one thing that just happened," I said to Mom at last.

Mom shifted to a more comfortable position. "This may all be coincidence, of course," she warned me. "I don't want to be overoptimistic, or have your hopes get too high for Rusty. But, and this is a big 'but,' horses as we know them today clearly have no resistance to this wicked virus. We've been assuming that it's something new—possibly a mutation or change in a milder virus that wouldn't have made horses so sick before. But then, why hasn't Zipper gotten it, too? Maybe we've been wrong and it's really a very *old* virus, one that hasn't been seen for thousands of years—like the true wild horse."

She paused, but I didn't say anything, and in a minute she went on.

"If the theory is right that it was a viral epidemic that destroyed the ancient herds of wild horses in the Americas, maybe the virus went into hiding along with a few scattered herds that survived—a handful of horses with immune systems developed enough to resist the virus. These horses might get sick but recover, because they were able to produce antibodies in their blood to fight the virus. Many of their foals, and their descendants through the centuries, could inherit this ability. And my guess is that Zipper is one of these horses."

I thought about it all for a while, looking out the darkened window, watching the fireflies spark in the apple orchard.

"If your guess *is* right about all this, and there are antibodies in Zipper's blood, could they cure Rusty? Permanently?" I said.

"No," Mom said. "All Zipper's antibodies can do is help Rusty while his system tries to make its own antibodies to fight the infection. It's possible that the fever has been killing the horses so quickly that their immune systems haven't had time to respond to the virus. But we can give Rusty more of Zipper's serum in a week or ten days. And then again, if he needs it. This won't hurt Zipper at all, and it may save Rusty. *If* my guess is right."

"Wow." I watched the fireflies a while longer.

"I can't be sure yet," Mom said cautiously. "We may find Rusty as sick as ever in the morning—"

"But you don't really think so," I said.

Mom smiled at me. "Science is knowledge, research, skill, and a little luck. It's possible we might have put them all together this afternoon."

I woke in the middle of the night, took a flashlight, and went out to the stable with Kim beside me. The moon had risen and everything was splashed with silver light. I tiptoed into the stable to look at Rusty. He was lying down, and though he didn't get up, he raised his head, pricked his ears, and nickered to me softly.

Mom was in the kitchen when I let myself quietly back into the house. "I heard you going out," she said with a smile. "I'd just come in from checking Rusty myself. He looks a great deal better, doesn't he?"

I didn't know what to say. I just hugged her fiercely. We made ourselves cocoa while Kim thumped his tail on the floor and begged for a marshmallow when I opened the package.

"You bet," I said to him. "All of us deserve marshmallows. Two." And I gave him a second one.

"You'll spoil that dog," Mom said automatically.

"He's a wonderful dog, and he's spoiled already," I said, which was always my answer. It was a perfectly good one, as far as Kim and I were concerned. And I knew Mom felt the same way.

Two days later, Rusty and Zipper were out in the pasture when Mom drove home. She came right out to the pasture gate where I was leaning with my chin on my folded arms, watching the horses. Kim was lying beside me in the grass, and our new calico kitten, Wendy, was sitting on top of one of the fence posts with her tail wrapped neatly around her paws.

"Rusty still looks fine, doesn't he?" Mom said. "And so does that funny little Zipper. She really never did show any signs of illness, did she? You're very observant, and you see her more than I do."

"I've watched her every single day," I said. "She hasn't even sneezed."

Mom nodded thoughtfully.

"So what does this really mean?" I turned to ask her. "I know horses are beginning to get sick in other parts of the country, some of the racetracks have closed, horse shows are being cancelled— Do we have the only two healthy horses left on the whole continent?"

"Not exactly," said Mom. "But things aren't getting any better."

"Zipper hasn't got enough blood to save hundreds of horses," I said wildly. I'd gotten a perfectly idiotic picture in my mind of long rows of desperate vets and owners ganging up to get Zipper for their own and draining all her precious blood like vampires. . . .

"No, of course not," Mom said. "But I've already been in touch with a few of the research labs. Usually I wouldn't dream of doing such a thing so soon. I'd wait until I was absolutely sure Rusty was going to live, and then try Zipper's serum on just a few more horses, at least. One surviving horse doesn't necessarily prove a thing. Rusty could be no more than a single happy exception. But if Zipper does have antibodies, and it sure looks that way to me, there isn't time to wait. I kept some of her blood samples and froze them—I sent them out this morning. The labs may well be able to use the new samples, along with Rusty's, to identify the virus, and then they'd have the beginning for a vaccine that could help other horses."

Zipper had snatched at a daisy and was capering in circles around Rusty with the flower in her mouth.

Mom smiled. "Scientists and doctors get a little cocky sometimes. So many new things discovered every day. Space and computers opening out into so many new frontiers. And we forget to look back a little, now and then, to what's still unknown in our own world around us."

Mom turned and threw her arms wide toward the soaring hills and mountains to the west. "This is such a vast country, such a vast continent—there must be hundreds of thousands of miles in North and South America where no one's ever been. Why *couldn't* there be a few small herds of wild horses left somewhere? And viruses science hasn't known about, or seen, for thousands of years? Oh, Kelly, just because no one has seen any wild horses in the mountains doesn't mean they don't exist. And I think . . . you know I do . . . I truly believe you found one when you found Zipper."

Chapter Twelve

It was almost more than my whirling mind could handle. I turned back toward the grazing horses in silence. Mom took Wendy into her arms and stroked her gently.

"Zipper will be famous if you tell," I said in a low voice. "People will come from everywhere. Even if they don't want her blood, they're going to want to look at her. Take pictures. Try to find out where I found her and where she came from. She's terribly shy and doesn't like fuss, Mom. She doesn't even like strange noises right here on the farm—"

"I haven't said a word about where I got the new blood samples," Mom said.

"People will know," I said. "They'll find out, you know they will, one way or another, if it turns out you really have found part of the answer to this awful sickness in Zipper."

Mom patted my arm. "Don't worry about it now," she said. "I may be nuts, you know, and may have made all of this up. Rusty might have gotten well on his own. We don't have any facts. Nothing's been proven."

"Not yet, maybe," I said. "But it would be a funny coincidence, Rusty's recovering the way he is, when every other horse that's gotten sick has died within a few days. For sure you would have heard if anyone else had saved a horse or a sick pony. Anywhere."

Mom patted me again and went into the house to change. I put my head down on my arms and watched the horses. Rusty had lost some weight during the hours he'd run that dreadful high fever, and his coat still looked ruffled and dry in spite of my grooming, but Mom assured me he'd soon look his usual shining self, if everything continued to go well.

Zipper's strange harsh coat never did shine very much, though I'd fussed with it for hours, once I'd been able to get the little horse used to the feel of the grooming brush. Her short black mane still stood on end, no matter how many times I'd dampened it and brushed it to one side.

There was no longer any question in my mind that she was different, a totally different kind of horse than any I'd ever known, and I'd seen a bunch.

Whenever Mom and Dad and I had traveled anywhere, we'd always stopped at different breeding farms and veterinary hospitals. I'd probably seen more kinds and breeds of horses than most people saw in a lifetime. Good ones and bad ones, tiny ponies and enormous, gentle draft horses. We'd seen mustangs running free in several open ranges, too, though Mom had made sure I understood they weren't true wild horses, but domestic horses that had run wild. Not the same thing at all. . . .

"Not the same thing at all," I said out loud. At the sound of my voice, both Rusty and Zipper trotted over toward me. I rubbed their heads gently, under their forelocks where they liked it best, until they both got bored at the same time and whirled away to set off on a happy gallop across the pasture.

The telephone started ringing off the hook three days later. Scientists with research labs were all calling Mom to talk to her about the mysterious virus and antibodies that had been finally discovered in the blood samples she'd sent.

Mom had been right. And every single person who called wanted to know where she'd gotten the samples.

Mom kept her promise. She didn't tell. "It puts me in an awkward position, of course," she said.

"The scientific training I've had is hard to deny. But the labs have what they need now, and I don't want, as a private person, to give away what I consider to be Zipper's secret."

Rusty looked better with every day that passed. Mom had no other horse patients in the valley. All of them had died, in spite of everything she and the other veterinarians had done.

Mom was kept busy with her farm animals. Though she missed her horse and pony patients, she'd always enjoyed taking care of the other animals, too, large or small. She was as happy helping a mother dog with her puppies as she was showing farmers the newest, safest systems of raising little pigs.

From what Mom heard from the labs, in strict confidence, their research looked extremely promising. And Mom and I knew, even if few other people did, that the scientists were close to developing a vaccine. Once they did, it would be safe to bring new horses back to the valley. The billion-dollar racing industry would be back in business, too. Though nothing would ever be exactly the same. Much as he missed them, Mr. Brewster could never afford to replace his own magnificent team of giant Clydesdales. Nothing could give Lori back her sweet bay Welsh mare, or bring Mark's gray Pennant back to him. But somehow there had to be a fresh beginning.

Not a lot of people came to our farm and happened to see our horses, but some did. And there were some awkward questions. Mom fudged the truth a little. She answered by saying we'd kept Rusty and his young companion well isolated from other horses, which was sure true enough, as far as it went. Since Mom had been the first to warn people to keep their horses and ponies at home, even before there was an official quarantine, this seemed to be enough to answer the questions in the valley.

No one who came to the farm ever saw Zipper clearly. At the first sight or sound of unfamiliar visitors, she'd drift to the far side of the pasture, where the ground sloped down to the stream, and hide in the moving shadows of the willow trees.

Summer slipped into fall. Zipper grew taller and more powerful every day. She wouldn't let me near her with a measuring stick or tape of any kind, so Mom and I could only guess at her exact height; Mom said Zipper would probably grow to the size of a large pony or a small horse.

"That fits my theory, too," Mom said, glowing with excitement. "The bones of ancient horses show them to have been *small* horses. What we'd call pony height today."

She shook her head with a smile. "It's a wonderful thought. Marvelous. It's nice we don't know *everything*, isn't it? Little herds of real wild horses, hiding their secret existence for thousands of years out there in the mountains . . . except for your incredible Zipper."

"Mom," I said nervously, "you promised."

Mom ruffled my hair with a gentle hand. "I won't tell. And we don't know whether or not I'm right, anyway. We'll probably never be able to know. Not for certain. I like thinking about it, though."

"And what about the virus?" I said. "It must be out there, too."

"Mystery indeed," Mom said. "Who knows for sure how all of this sickness started so suddenly this year? But I have a theory about that, too. Along with the wild horses and virus we're only guessing about, there must have been small animals in isolated pockets of the mountains. Anything from rabbits to mice. They wouldn't be sick themselves, but they could be carriers of this virus.

"The whole Northwest had such a crazy winter. We know you found Zipper where a crack broke through one mountain. It's only sensible to believe that little animals came through either there or in a lot of other possible places, other fresh gaps somewhere in the mountain ranges after those fierce storms. They could have brought the virus with them, and then mosquitoes or flies could have started spreading it far and wide. Imagine. An Ice Age virus—small wonder today's horses couldn't handle it."

"What about Zipper?" I finally asked the question I'd been worrying about for weeks. "Could she have been the one to bring the virus out of the mountain?"

"She was well when you brought her here," Mom said. "And she's not a carrier, like the horses or ponies that look healthy but sometimes are carriers of viruses like swamp fever. I had this checked out by one of the labs. She must have been exposed to the virus at some time and recovered—that's why she'd have the antibodies. Newborn foals get antibodies from their mothers' milk, but those are temporary. Zipper was old enough when you found her to have developed her own immunity."

Mom gave a slightly embarrassed laugh, trying to make light of her theories, but I knew she truly believed what she said. Whether she could prove it or not.

It was always interesting and fun to work with Zipper. She would follow me when I walked in the pasture and let me brush her in her stall. She learned to accept a carrot or apple from my hand without trying to bite. She let me put my arm over her shoulder, though she never learned to be led. She trusted me in so many ways, but she wouldn't let me put a halter on her head or pick up her feet.

Mom offered suggestions and advice, but eventually we both decided Zipper had a tremendous fear of feeling trapped. Whether it was her genuine wildness, or the memory of the time she'd spent tangled in the vines near her injured mother, there was no way of knowing.

Chapter Thirteen

The apples were turning scarlet on the orchard trees, and bright autumn colors were flaming in the woods beyond the pasture.

School started. It was good to see all my friends again. The summer had been such a strange, unhappy time for most of us. Even the 4-H Club meetings had been cancelled. No one had wanted to hear talks about bridles and saddles, or to watch films about horses, when so many everywhere were gone.

At school we had other things to share and to talk about, new teachers to meet, and new subjects to handle. I was accepted into the glee club, which was exciting. We started practicing songs for the Thanksgiving holiday right away.

Mom was picking tomatoes in the vegetable garden one soft golden afternoon when a long, dark car swept down our bumpy driveway. The car had New York license plates. Mom dusted her hands on her jeans and went over to see who it was and what they wanted.

"Mr. Stevenson would like to see Dr. Caldwell, please," the driver said to Mom. He looked stiff and stern in his gray chauffeur's uniform, but Mom just smiled her usual polite smile. I had been picking late raspberries for our dessert that night. Since the bushes grew near the garden fence, I stopped to watch and listen.

"I'm Dr. Caldwell," Mom said. "How may I help you?"

The chauffeur spoke to the people in the back of the car, which had dark-tinted windows so no one could see in. They gave the huge car a brooding, sinister look. The chauffeur opened the back door and a man and a woman got out, dressed the way I hadn't seen people dress since we'd left New York.

To my surprise, because Mom usually was more hospitable, she didn't invite the strangers into the house. They spoke in low voices beside the car and, much as I strained to listen, I couldn't make out what they were saying at first.

"I'm sorry." I finally was able to hear Mom's voice as she spoke more sharply and clearly. "I can't help you."

"You mean you won't." The man's voice was raised, too.

Mom's voice was stiff and cold. "The blood samples have been made available to all the research labs that have asked for them. I have no intention of keeping any of these findings to myself. If I was fortunate enough to discover something that might possibly be of some help against this terrible disease, it seemed the least I could do was to share it so a protective vaccine could be made as soon as possible. I never had any intention of turning my luck into a personal gold mine."

There was more, but I went back to picking raspberries. Mom soon came back to the garden, slapping the gate shut with unusual violence.

"They were from one of the biggest pharmaceutical companies," Mom reported. Her face was flushed with anger. "They wanted an exclusive on 'my' serum, even though it was one of the smaller labs that really identified the virus and has done most of the preliminary work. Never mind, they're not going to get anything from me. Few ordinary horse owners would be able to afford the vaccine once one of those big companies priced it out of orbit, as they've done with so many fancy new antibiotics and vaccines. What nonsense. Can you imagine having gone through all we did, and then letting only the wealthier owners afford the vaccine?"

She placed a few more ripe tomatoes gently into her basket. "I don't even know how these people tracked the original samples back to me, anyway. The labs all promised secrecy, but I guess there was a leak. Not that it matters." She yanked ferociously at a stubborn weed.

She threw the weed to the ground, set her hands on her hips, put her head back and laughed. "They offered me a bundle of money and a royalty on every bottle sold, and said they'd be glad to name the new vaccine after me. Little did they know they'd have to call it the Zipper Vaccine. Doesn't sound grand enough, does it?"

I laughed, too, but with an inner dull feeling of dread. The image of cars lining up in our driveway, filled with people wanting to drain blood from Zipper, like vampires, came back to me again.

Rusty and Zipper continued to flourish, even after school started, without my anxious eye on them every minute. The word about the new vaccine was more optimistic than ever. There'd been excellent results with test horses in several different parts of the country where the virus still was spreading. Mom told me it might take anywhere from six months to two years for a reliable vaccine to come from all of this, but at least and at last there was a light at the end of the tunnel.

Dad wrote that he'd be home for Christmas. Wonderful news. Mom and I went for walks just beyond the pasture fence and found a perfect little fir tree struggling to grow under the branches of another. It would never get anywhere in the shadow of the bigger evergreen tree, so we marked the small one by fastening a strip of white cloth on its top. It would be our Christmas tree. Mom tied the cloth in a floppy bow and left long streamers on it, hoping this might discourage the deer from eating too much of the small tree. The deer loved to nibble at the soft top shoots of little firs, even though there were plenty of other things for them to eat everywhere around them.

"We'll let the deer have some of the apples in the orchard, instead," said Mom as she stood back to admire the bow and the tree.

I laughed—the lovely deer always helped themselves to all the apples they could reach, anyway. Even Kim had accepted them as part of our farm and never chased them away. We would watch the deer together in the evenings when they came down to the orchard, balancing themselves on their slim hind legs while they picked apples delicately from the branches of the trees above their heads.

I rode Rusty almost every afternoon, staying in the big fenced pasture so that Zipper could romp along with us. I still wasn't sure what might happen if I tried to leave her shut up in her stall alone while I rode out on Rusty without her. And I was afraid to let her run free.

Another big car came to our house a week later. Again Mom turned it away, but it was followed the next morning by two others.

This time Mom was out on a call. It was Sunday morning, but there are no days of rest for farm veterinarians—one of the Brewsters' cows needed help with her calf and Mom had left twenty minutes before.

The cars started to go around the house, following the track to the stable. Kim and I ran out to stop them. I told the drivers crisply that Mom was out, I didn't know how long it would be before she got back, and suggested firmly she should be called on the telephone in the evening for an appointment. Kim showed his teeth and growled. It was all very dramatic, and I felt ten feet tall until after they'd gone. Then I sat down on the ground where I was, held Kim, and cried into his soft white ruff. There was an uneasy feeling of threat in the air—not to me, but to Zipper.

Rusty, curious and friendly as always, had come to the pasture fence when he'd heard the car driving close to the stable. Zipper had fled to the far corner of the pasture. As her coat had thickened for the coming winter, the russet shading of color over her back had turned to a quiet brown. The light, mealy shadings of tan on her muzzle and stomach and upper legs had lightened. The black zipper marks on the pale dusty background color, along with her black lower legs, mane, and tail, stood out in sharper contrast. Up close, her colors and shadings made her look like a circus parade, but at a distance, she faded into the patterns of sunlight and shadow and blended with the colors of the browning grass in the field and the first falling leaves of the trees.

I called to her and she came out of the shadows, hesitantly, with her funny little head held high and her black eyes gleaming suspiciously. "It's okay, Zip," I said to her fondly. "They're gone."

Chapter Fourteen

"But they won't stay away, Mom. You know they won't," I said that night after dinner.

Mom sighed and ran her hands through her hair. Two letters lay on the kitchen table, both of them from veterinary journals asking Mom to write articles for them about how and where she'd found the original blood samples.

"No one need ever know about Zipper," Mom said firmly. "I'm certainly not going to say a word about her in any articles. And we're not about to tell anyone we consider her a true wild horse. Who'd believe us, in any event? It's only a far-out theory of our own, anyway, no scientific proof whatsoever, so why should anyone listen or care? All that matters is that the vaccine is showing promise. The heck with the rest of it."

"People will want to know how you found those first blood samples with the antibodies. And where. You know that," I said, almost angrily. "Mom, you're *not* being realistic."

"Things will settle down in a little while," Mom said comfortably. "Once a vaccine is available, everyone quickly takes it for granted. People forget how bad things were without it. You're too young to remember the discovery of the polio vaccine—do you know who Dr. Salk is? Dr. Sabin? Smallpox is almost entirely gone now, too, all over the world, because of vaccines. How many young veterinarians today have seen a case of distemper in a puppy? Distemper alone used to kill whole kennels full of adult dogs and puppies at a time. And encephalitis in horses, for another example—three different kinds have been identified, and we inoculate our horses and ponies against them every year. More people complain about the bills than ever stop to think what a threat these were before the vaccines. Who stops to wonder who developed any of these precious vaccines, or who first identified each virus?"

It seemed for a little while that Mom was right. I was the only person in the world who knew where Zipper had been found, and I wasn't going to talk about her. Anyway, as Mom said, who would be ready to believe she was a true wild horse, separated along with her mother somehow from a hidden herd high in the mountains? It was silly to worry. Nobody would. It sounded like a spaced-out fantasy, at best.

We heard it on the radio first, and then on television, and then the newspapers carried headlines. A breeder had ducked the quarantine on horses in North America by flying a stallion out of the country. And the horse had just died of "an unidentified virus" in England.

Because of the flow of information among veterinarians all over the world, we soon knew the horse that had been stabled next to him had begun to run a very high fever.

If the vicious virus spread, as it was sure to do, every horse and pony in England would be endangered. Certainly all the horses on the breeding farm where the stallion had died were doomed.

The new vaccine was still considered to be in the experimental stage, but there was no hesitation. The lab working with the more advanced vaccine sent a few vials of the treasured stuff on a special plane to England. And the inoculated horses, thanks to Zipper, lived.

Mom was swamped with calls. The phone never seemed to stop ringing. A national news magazine wanted an exclusive interview. This was human interest stuff that readers loved: small country vet, savior of horses in all parts of the world through her mysterious discovery. One magazine found a photograph of Mom in her college yearbook and ran it on their science page.

"You're going to be rich and famous," I teased Mom, "in spite of yourself." But I wasn't either amused or impressed. And neither was Mom.

The pressures built. Because of Mom's refusal to have so much as an interviewer or a photographer on the place, the air of mystery grew and grew. And the magazines and papers and even the television people became more and more anxious and curious.

"All of this to protect one strange-looking young horse that's probably no more than a throwback to a strayed mustang," Mom said. "The whole thing has become ridiculous."

Her remark scared me half to death until I realized that she was still convinced that Zipper was truly a wild horse.

"No proof," Mom kept repeating. "There's absolutely no proof I'm right and it's a mad idea, to begin with." But, at the same time, I saw she was determined not to allow a photographer onto the farm under any circumstances.

"Someone who knows enough might see a photo

of Zipper," she said. "Most people wouldn't notice what we've seen in her. But it's only going to take one analytical mind—one photograph to catch the eye of someone with the right kind of background. A zoologist, or a geologist, or an expert in prehistoric art. Someone who might get curious and put basic two and two together. We must be so careful. I don't want to run the risk of *anyone* identifying Zipper. If there are small herds of true wild horses still out there in the mountains, they *must* be protected."

I shuddered. I didn't want eager scientific experts invading our farm, either. Zipper hated strangers and was terrified of unfamiliar sounds. I could imagine cameras clicking and snapping, driving her into fierce panic. Enthusiastic amateur expeditions crawling over the mountain. Helicopters, maybe, searching, with their battering noises, for the spot where I'd found Zipper. . . .

Again I spent an evening, dazed with wonder, curled up by the fireplace in my favorite chair with the books Mom had shown me on prehistoric art. The next day, during all my free time and in study periods at school, I went to the library and took from the shelf another small book full of glowing color illustrations of the Ice Age paintings on the walls in the caves of France and Spain.

I studied them until the pictures seemed to dance on their pages, going over them again and again. I even missed glee club practice. There were paintings of deer and reindeer with graceful, wide-spreading antlers. There were dynamic shapes of powerful bison, looking just the same as they did today. There were drawings and paintings of cattle with splendid curved horns. And, above all, and to me the most beautiful, there were the paintings of the horses, standing and galloping, running and playing. And almost every single one of them was shaded and marked with precise detail, just exactly the way Zipper was in my own stable at home.

I returned the book reluctantly at the end of the day—we couldn't take art books home from the library—thanked the librarian, and went outside to catch the bus home. I blinked in the afternoon sunlight and rubbed my eyes. Lori, sitting beside me on the bus, asked sympathetically if I felt okay. I told her I just had a headache, nothing much, but I was tired and glad tomorrow was Saturday. It helped to explain why I didn't want to talk during the ride home.

Chapter Fifteen

I needed to do a lot of thinking.

There were all kinds of sandy dun horses in many breeds. Big ones and little ones, all of them the same basic dusty earth colors of Zipper. Most duns had the black stripes down their backs, too, and black legs, manes, and tails. Some of them even had faint black tracings above their knees and hocks.

That made sense, and could explain Zipper. She might well be a dun mustang foal, even though I knew, at the same time, there'd been no mustangs in our part of the country for years.

There was no use trying to go on kidding myself, much as I wanted to. No ordinary horse or pony, either in real life or in modern pictures, looked anything like Zipper. Her shaded patterns of browns and pale tans were not standard dun colors. And her conformation was totally different. Her black mane was short and stood on end; it never had grown out to be a full mane. Her black, oval eyes, the rim of black around her ears and lips, her stocky little body with its wide, short neck and distinctive head . . . . Too many pieces matched.

I didn't want Zipper to be so rare and special; she was already special to me. I didn't want Mom to be right. But what she said made sense. And the older Zipper got, the more she looked like the paintings from the walls of the Ice Age caves.

That evening, after dinner, I looked again at the pictures in Mom's books. Rock engravings, lots of them. More photographs of statues of little horses carved from ivory or reindeer antlers. And the splendor of the cave paintings. . . . I held one book open on my lap to a prehistoric portrait of a horse's head, discovered on the walls of a cave in France. Zipper looked right back at me from the shining black eyes in the picture.

I closed the book gently. I knew what I had to do.

I set my alarm for five o'clock the next morning. The sun wasn't up and there'd been a sharp frost during the night. I found my down jacket where I'd put it at the back of the closet in the hall, and I snuggled into it gratefully as I called softly to Kim and shut the kitchen door behind me.

I left a note for Mom on the kitchen table. "I'm all right," it said. "I'll be back by supper time."

I hoped she wouldn't worry, but I didn't want to say anything more.

Dim light was beginning to soften the dark sky in the east—just enough to see by as I went to the stable. Rusty and Zipper were surprised to see me so early. But they were always glad to have their breakfast. I gave them each a light feeding of grain. I sat at the open stable door while they ate, watching the day come to life around me as the light brightened. The blurred shadows of the deer in the orchard took shape and turned to the color of glowing amber, and the ripe apples to dark shining rubies, as the sun rose higher.

Kim sat close beside me, watching with me, and his warmth was comforting.

His black coat began to brighten with blue highlights, and his white ruff and paws sparkled as the first rays of sun came into the stable yard.

It was time to go.

I bridled Rusty and checked the pockets of my jacket. This time I had my strong red pocket knife with me, in case I needed it, and a small pair of good binoculars. I snapped my pockets shut and opened Zipper's stall door.

For the first time since she'd come to us, we went

out the front door of the stable and through the open gate.

I wiggled my way up on Rusty's back, straightened the reins, and squeezed his sides with my legs, turning his head toward the open fields and the mountain beyond.

Zipper bucked and played along beside Rusty as I rode him past the orchard and onto what was left of the bridle path that led through the trees. In some places the path was too narrow for Zipper to stay beside Rusty, but she was content then to follow close behind him.

The bridle path hadn't been used during the past summer. New growth had spread over it in many places, but we pushed our way through without too much trouble. I ducked low on Rusty's neck when overgrown tree branches threatened to pull me off the horse's back. He moved forward quietly, but clearly he was enjoying being out in the woods again after so many months of confinement behind his pasture fence.

The woods were a riot of autumn color with the deep green of pine trees accenting the bright crimsons and golds around them. The sun rose higher, and the sky, where I could see it through the tree branches, was crystal blue. White pockets of frost had scattered their patterns in low places, but they were quickly disappearing as the day grew warmer.

The path turned to the left and sloped upward. Soon we were at the place where Rusty had stopped so many weeks—months—ago on the morning I'd found Zipper. It seemed a lifetime to me. I pressed him forward.

The footing grew rougher. We made our way around the fallen boulders and tree trunks. The towering rock ledge was beside us, half hidden now by low bushes and fresh vines. The gullies carved into the earth by the rioting spring floods were filled with growing things, but somehow we found our way through, always moving higher. There were deer paths here, and I rode along them whenever the main bridle path disappeared under rock slides and tree trunks, keeping my bearings by following the slope as it rose in front of us.

We'd been out on the mountain for almost two hours. I stopped to give Rusty another chance to catch his breath and rest for a few minutes. I pulled the small binoculars from the pocket of my jacket and raised them to my eyes.

At first all I could see were thick trees and bushes and vines everywhere. But I fiddled with the focus of the lenses. I was as positive as I'd ever been about anything in my life that if I had the patience, I'd find what I was looking for.

It took a while. Rusty was beginning to toss his head impatiently, and Zipper was bumping him with her nose, bored with going nowhere and looking for mischief. Kim waited in front of us, watching me silently with his head cocked to one side.

I found at last what I'd been so sure was there. A narrow, ragged gap in the high stone ledge. Though small shrubs and vines already had grown to cover most of it, the shadowed stone stood out in jagged outline against the sky.

For the first time, I didn't know what to do next. Rusty was as surefooted as any horse could be, but the gray rock ledge was nearly vertical and towered high over our heads.

I didn't dare get off and try to leave Rusty tied to a tree. I was afraid he'd break his bridle and run off again. I looked around me anxiously and finally spotted a place that had been a narrow mudslide or an avalanche path during the past winter. It had settled now and was already covered with tufts of grass and low-growing vines and bushes. But it led directly to the high gap in the ledge. It would have to do.

"Come on, Rusty," I said to the willing horse. He turned at the touch of my heel and tackled the slope.

I gave him all the rein length I could to free his head. Snorting a little, he picked his way around the rocks and bushes and through the tangles of vines, with Zipper trotting behind.

Chapter Sixteen

Blackberry bushes tore at my jeans. Wild grapevines twisted everywhere, and brambles, with leaves turned to scarlet, snatched at our legs. Rusty crushed sassafras under his strong hoofs, and its fragrance rose around us to mix with the deep, smoky scent of pine. Huge oaks and maples arched their branches high over our heads in glowing crimson and copper colors, and aspens shimmered with lemon-bright light on their leaves.

Zipper skipped behind us, following every twist and turn Rusty made, like a little red ball fastened to a toy paddle by an invisible elastic thread. Kim slipped along at the back like a smooth, dark shadow. If there'd been anyone to see us, we'd have looked like a miniature parade.

We reached the crest at last. I stopped Rusty, drew

a deep breath of relief, and let it out quickly in a soundless whistle. Even though I'd pictured in my mind a hidden valley, it was even more beautiful than I'd imagined.

Just in front of us, a torrent of deep-gold wildflowers spilled down the sharp slope to a meadow beyond. To the right, taller fringed blossoms of rich purple led down to the vivid greens and bronze of the autumn meadow grass and to a stream foaming white over low waterfalls until the water spread into a quiet dark pool, reflecting the light of the deep blue sky.

The meadow stretched out to a thick line of forest trees in flaming fall colors. Still farther beyond, another and far higher range of lavender-shaded mountains soared into an outline of snowy peaks.

The meadow, wide as it was, was silent in the soft autumn sunlight. I could only see four Canada geese quietly dipping their beaks into the pool. They hardly made so much as a ripple.

Everything else was still. I fussed with the binoculars. My hands were shaking a little, which made focusing difficult. There was certainly no sign I could find that any lumber company had cut or marked a single tree anywhere here, no trace of so much as a little-used ski trail or hiking path. It wasn't hard to believe that no one, ever, had been here before me.

I glanced over at Kim. He was sitting motionless on the crest of the ledge, his ears pricked forward, looking intently at the far side of the meadow.

I swung the binoculars to the back line of trees, and I saw them at last. There must have been ten or twelve of them. I couldn't be sure, because they were standing in the changing patterns of sunlight and shadow near the trees, which made them hard to count with any certainty. But there were several of them there, all with their heads turned toward me, every one of them a small and sandy brown horse. They looked as though they had stepped out from the Ice Age paintings of the cave walls. And every little horse looked exactly like Zipper.

"That's it, then," I said in a quiet voice to Rusty.

I rode him to one side of the ragged path and held him still. Mom had been right, though no one in the world except me would probably ever believe her. But I knew what I'd seen, and it was enough.

Zipper pranced past Rusty impatiently and froze at the top edge of the cracked ledge. I saw she was trembling—she'd caught the scent of the other horses. She whinnied loudly. One of the little brown horses answered and moved a few steps out of the shadows into the open meadow.

Zipper hesitated. She turned her head toward Rusty and then looked up at me.

"Good-by, Zipper," I said in a shaking voice.

Almost as though I'd given her permission, Zipper flicked her short black tail, set her little ears determinedly, and started to scramble down the far side of the slope, through the tumbled rocks and wildflowers that led to the meadow.

Rusty didn't nicker to her, though I'd thought he might. Kim raised one white paw. He was quivering, but he didn't move, even when Zipper bounced into her funny short gallop when she reached the open meadow and raced away from us, toward the other horses.

Partway across the meadow, she slid to a stop and whirled to face Rusty, Kim, and me. She half reared. She whinnied once more, and another of the small brown horses answered her. Zipper struck the ground once with a foreleg, hesitated, and then spun away. We watched silently as she became smaller and smaller in the distance, galloping away from us toward the herd of waiting horses.

A tall white bird rose quietly from the shore of the stream and drifted away on unhurried wings. There were no sounds at all any longer. It was a silence of total isolation and undisturbed peace.

I blinked the tears from my eyes, and the little dun horses were gone. All of them. They'd faded back into the shadows as though they'd never existed at all. And Zipper had disappeared with them. She was back where she belonged.

I turned away and put the binoculars back in my pocket. I got off Rusty and, holding onto the reins, pulled the ends of some vines across the top of the broken ledge. Most of the fallen stones were too heavy for me to lift, but I moved the ones I could and stuffed a few small shrubs, with the earth clinging to their roots, into the pockets the stones had made. Even without my efforts, I knew, the underbrush and growth of new young trees would hide every trace of the broken ledge within a very short time. It wouldn't be long before this spot would be invisible, and impassable, again.

I climbed on a fallen tree trunk and struggled wearily onto Rusty's back. I glanced over my shoulder, just once, at the towering rock ledge. Then I turned Rusty to the steep, rocky pathway leading back the way we'd come, down the eastern slope of the mountainside.

"Come on, Kim," I said in a low voice to the waiting dog. "It's time for us to go home."

Mom was right about the rest of it, too. The fuss about Zipper's vaccine died down quickly as the world soon took it for granted. Early in November, though, we found a photographer sneaking down to our stable through the back pasture and, much to his surprise, invited him in. All he found was Rusty, round and well and shaggy with his winter coat. The other stall was empty.

"That's it?" said the photographer, looking terribly disappointed.

"That's it," said Mom. I said nothing at all. I stood with one hand on Kim's head as he sat beside me, leaning against my leg, while the calico kitten played between his front paws. The only sound in the stable was the whisper of the kitten's paws as she chased a scrap of hay around Kim.

The photographer sighed and put his camera away. "It sounded like a heck of a story," he said. "Genius lady scientist working with mysterious virus. . . . My editor thought you'd have a big secret laboratory, at the very least. With a dozen horses or more. And a whole building full of exotic equipment."

"I'm only a country vet," said Mom. "There's no story here."

She was right again. There was no story in our little stable any longer. And we weren't going to tell him, or anyone else who came, where the story had gone.